SCOTT STARKEY

THE CALL of THE BULLY

A Rodney Rathbone Novel

A PAULA WISEMAN BOOK
Simon & Schuster Books for Young Readers
New York London Toronto Sydney New Delhi

ALSO BY SCOTT STARKEY

How to Beat the Bully Without Really Trying

SIMON & SCHUSTER BOOKS FOR YOUNG READERS
An imprint of Simon & Schuster Children's Publishing Division
1230 Avenue of the Americas, New York, New York 10020
SIMON & SCHUSTER BOOKS FOR YOUNG READERS
is a trademark of Simon & Schuster, Inc.
For information about special discounts for bulk purchases,
please contact Simon & Schuster Special Sales at 1-866-506-1949
or business@simonandschuster.com.
The Simon & Schuster Speakers Bureau can bring authors to
your live event. For more information or to book an event, contact
the Simon & Schuster Speakers Bureau at 1-866-248-3049 or
visit our website at www.simonspeakers.com.
Book design by Krista Vossen
The text for this book is set in Bembo Std.
Manufactured in the United States of America
1112 FFG
2 4 6 8 10 9 8 7 5 3 1
Library of Congress Cataloging-in-Publication Data
Starkey, Scott.
The call of the bully : a Rodney Rathbone novel / Scott Starkey.—First edition.
p. cm
Summary: Stuck at Camp Wy-Mee, cowardly Rodney Rathbone is forced to try to
make friends and finds himself once again in the unlikely roll of camp hero.
ISBN 978-1-4424-5674-7 (hardcover)
ISBN 978-1-4424-5676-1 (eBook)
[1. Camps—Fiction. 2. Bullies—Fiction. 3. Friendship—Fiction.
4. Humorous stories.] I. Title.
PZ7.S7952Cal 2013
[Fic]—dc23
2012039444

Dedicated to my daughter, Brooke

Acknowledgments

Most authors have people who help them along the way and I am no exception. Once again, I thank Paula Wiseman and everyone else at Simon & Schuster for their belief in me. I thank my wife, Judy, for all her support, ideas, and for helping me find time in our busy schedules to write. I also thank all the kids out there who enjoyed Rodney's first adventure. Your letters keep me very motivated!

Lastly, I want to thank my friend Lloyd Singer. It was his encouragement that got me writing years ago, his criticism that made me a stronger writer, and his edits that helped make this a book I'm very proud to share with you.

CONTENTS

Chapter 1

THE VAN RIDE

Through the van window I watched Mrs. Lutzkraut shake my dad's hand and give my mom a big hug. Then she turned to wave good-bye to me. On her face was a smile—a perfectly evil grin. I'd never seen her look so happy. My demented former teacher and I shared a secret, you see. I was about to die, and she knew it.

The cause of my inevitable end, Josh, was on the van with me. And as my parents and Mrs. Lutzkraut disappeared in the distance, I shifted my eyes to watch him. He sat across the aisle, glaring out the window. There was one other kid in the back of the van, but he had been asleep when Josh and I climbed on. I doubted he would come to my rescue when Josh attacked.

An old, familiar feeling of terror began to rise from my stomach. There was no doubt in my mind that Josh was about to crush me. I mean, that had been his main goal the entire school year. Now all that separated us was about six feet. I rubbed my sweaty palms on my shorts and stared out the window.

Maybe Josh would wait until we got to summer camp before killing me. That meant I had about two hours left to enjoy life. Only there was nothing to enjoy and nothing happy to think about. I was being shipped off to someplace called Camp Wy-Mee with my worst enemy. For eight weeks!

Oh yes, Mrs. Lutzkraut had a lot to be smiling about this afternoon. She had tricked my parents—and Josh's parents—into thinking summer camp was the best thing in the world. Josh hadn't looked too pleased about it either. I shifted in the uncomfortable van seat and let my eyes wander in his direction. Big mistake.

"Forget about me, Rathbone?"

He must have been staring at me the whole time. This was it. I tried to answer but nothing came out.

"Yeah, Rathbone, you ain't that tough. I could see you were real scared at graduation. I was a fool all year, thinkin' you were tough. This time nothing's saving you. Punching you's gonna be like Christmas morning. Guess that makes me Santa."

I didn't understand his logic, but I understood what it meant when his legs shifted into the aisle. I raised my arms in a feeble attempt to block the incoming buffalo stampede.

Vroom! The engine revved and I could feel tires skidding on sand. The van swerved, knocking Josh off-balance. I watched as Santa banged his head on the floor.

"You there!" the driver hollered.

"Me?" I squeaked.

"Yeah, you." I could see the driver's grizzled face and dark eyes in the big rearview mirror. "Help that kid up." Josh was rolling around in the aisle, dazed and holding his head. "Go on, put him in a seat."

I looked closer at the driver. He wore a ripped tank top and had a big bushy beard. "Do I have to?" I asked.

"Do it!" the driver ordered.

I reached down to grab Josh under the arms just as the driver turned his attention back to the road. The van swerved violently, knocking *me* off-balance. I landed with a crunch, right on top of Josh.

"No more, no more," he whimpered. "I'll behave, Rodney, I promise. Just leave me alone."

I backed away and watched him climb into his seat, where he curled up into a ball. My jaw hung low, shocked. There was no tougher kid than Josh. He was like twice my size. Thanks to the van driver's horrible driving, Josh had been knocked down before he could even throw a punch. Maybe my amazing run of luck from the school year wasn't over. Not just yet, anyway.

Chapter 2

MY NEW BEAST FRIEND

Josh had been quiet for about an hour as we drove along—probably wondering how I always got the best of him. "You look pretty runty," he finally muttered. "I don't get it. How come you fight good?"

"Well," I corrected him. My mom's constant grammar reminders were rubbing off on me.

"Huh?"

"How come you fight *well.*"

"Oh, I guess because I'm tough." I rolled my eyes. He continued, "But how come you fight good too, Rathbone?"

He was still holding the side of his head. I relaxed a little and my big mouth kicked into gear. "For starters, I have natural killer instincts. Combine that with years of high-intensity combat training, not to mention . . ."

He was looking at me intently now, but I'm not sure how much was reaching his brain. Finally he just smiled and said, "Yeah, fighting's good."

It was the first time I'd ever seen him smile, not counting when he inflicted pain on some poor kid. He turned and looked out the window for a moment. "You know," he continued, "I beat up over a hundred kids and never lost one fight. Then you beat me up two times. Plus today. That makes . . ."

The higher math was too much for him. "Three," I informed him.

"Yeah, whatever. It's just, I still can't believe it." He sounded both disappointed and respectful. "Before you came along I did whatever I wanted, took whatever I wanted, beat up whoever I wanted, did whatever I wanted . . ."

I couldn't believe we were having a conversation. A weird, creepy conversation, but a conversation. Usually he just grunted or told me how he was going to knock my face apart. "I never wanted to ruin your year," I explained, "but you're the one who picked a fight. You play with fire, you get burned."

"You like fire, too?"

Boy, this kid was thick. "Yeah, fire's pretty cool," I agreed. I was willing to play along if it meant keeping his hands off my neck.

"I love fire! I got a lighter. You want to help me light this seat on fire?"

"I think we should probably leave the seats alone. You see," I explained, "we're traveling in the van that you want to set fire to."

He seemed to contemplate that for a minute.

"Anyway, Rathbone, you're actually not that bad. Hey, check this out." With a dumb grin etched on his lips, he began punching the back of the seat in front of him. I, on the other hand, wrestled with the vision of bunk beds burning in my cabin.

I gazed out the window and watched the Ohio countryside pass by, each mile taking me farther from home. I was miserable. Sure, I had dodged a bullet with Josh, but you have to understand the incredible school year that was still fresh in my mind. When it started, I was the new kid in town, afraid of getting pounded to a pulp at school. Then, through pure luck, I became Mr. Popular. Hero of the Town. Czar of the Playground! I met Rishi, Slim, and Dave—the three best friends I'd ever had. No group could make me laugh so hard. Rishi was the big talker and had outlined a million awesome things for us to do this summer. None of it would be happening now—with me, at least.

As the van zoomed down the highway I thought about something else that was making me miserable. I had left behind my girlfriend, Jessica. We'd been "officially" going out for about twenty minutes when my parents dropped the camp bomb.

"Hey, Rodney," Josh suddenly called out from his seat.

Whatever he was about to say, no matter how dumb, I actually welcomed the distraction. Anything to get my mind off Jessica! "Yeah?" I asked.

"You going out with Jessica?"

Evidently I was traveling with the Amazing Moron Mind Reader. "I don't want to talk about it," I answered.

"Uh, okay, so you going out with her?"

His words hurt more than his fists ever could. I didn't know if being apart from her was going to end our relationship. I sighed. "Listen, she's not happy with me going away and all."

"No? Don't feel bad, though."

"Why not?" I asked.

"Because she's real pretty. She'll find a new boyfriend in no time."

I stared at the gorilla sitting next to me. "How's that supposed to make me feel better?"

"Huh? Oh, I guess I got that backward. Yeah, you should feel bad. Hey, driver, I gotta take a whiz!"

I watched the driver's face in the rearview mirror. He was chewing on a toothpick. "We'll be at camp soon."

He had introduced himself as . . . hmm, was it Grizzly Bob, or Creepy Bill, or Smelly Stan? . . . No, it was Survival Steve. He had a bushy beard and a deep voice, and his eyes were dark and menacing. Worst of all, he wore a big hunting knife on his leather belt.

Josh didn't seem to notice or care. "I gotta go so bad I could fill a pool!"

Survival Steve's eyebrows rose for a moment. "We'll take a shortcut, down the old logger road. You can go on

the side somewhere. It'll save time and it's good scenery."
He banked down the next exit ramp off the highway,
turned left, and eventually made a right on a dirt road.

I'm not sure you could really call it a road. After a
while the trees and branches closed in and began whacking the sides of the van. Josh's face was scrunched up
and he was holding himself. I moved farther away, not
wanting to get sprayed by a yellow geyser. "Pull over!"
he yelled.

Survival Steve said, "Hold your water. That looks
like a good spot up ahead." He brought the van to a
stop. "Guess you can go . . ."

Josh didn't wait. He bolted out the door and off into
the woods.

"All right, how about you two?"

I needed to go, though probably not as badly as
Josh. I could hear him moaning off in the woods. As
I angled toward the door I noticed that the kid in the
back was awake now. He shook his head, and his eyes
looked frightened under the brim of his red baseball
cap. I couldn't blame him for being nervous, considering we were stopped in the middle of nowhere. After
glancing around, he curled up and pulled his hat down
further.

I climbed out and walked a few paces away from the
van into the woods. The dark pine forest smelled thick
and sweet, and the air hung heavy. It was real quiet and
eerie. I noticed that the sun was already setting behind

the tallest trees. As I finished my business, I shivered and realized I couldn't wait to get back in the van.

"Beautiful, ain't it?" It was Survival Steve.

"I guess," I answered.

"Yup, these woods are something special. I once lived in them by myself for three years. Killed a moose with only a rock, like this one. Moose liver, now that's tasty stuff."

I looked back at him. The word *insane* flashed through my mind.

"What's your name?" he asked.

"Rodney."

"Rodney, check this out!" He picked up the rock and flung it right at a tree. A huge section of bark shattered from the trunk. "Aim still perfect." He grinned. "Nothing beats a good stone." I was too scared to comment. "Rodney, you come by my shack at camp, I'll teach you to throw a stone like that, better yet I'll show you how to use a bow and arrow."

Avoid all shacks this summer, I thought as we returned to the van.

"You!" Steve hollered at Josh, who was back from the woods. "Go get that other kid and see if he wants a soda."

Josh made an evil grin and I knew what was coming as he climbed inside the van. The next sound I heard would be . . .

Thwack!

"Owwwww!" screamed the unsuspecting kid. "Why'd you hit me?"

"Driver said to," Josh declared.

"Huh?"

Whack!

"Owwwww!"

The poor kid tumbled out of the van. "Where the heck are we?" he asked, moving away from Josh, who had jumped down behind him. Survival Steve stepped forward, rock in hand. The kid's lips started quivering as he backed away, a look of panic building on his face.

"Guess I'll open this sucker up with Old Reliable," Survivor Steve announced. The rock raised, ready to strike.

"Whooaahhhh!" The kid was off like a shot, tearing into the woods.

"I was only talking about this can of soda," Steve laughed. "The opener thing broke. Now I gotta go get that scaredy-cat. You two, wait here."

I suddenly found myself alone with Josh in the middle of nowhere. Thank God we had "bonded" on the van, because instead of threatening me like he'd done in the past, he told me a story about a time he had punched his friend Toby in the face at school. We were both laughing when Survival Steve came trudging back from the woods.

"All right, we got problems. That kid ran off. Far. We're all going to have to go find him. We better spread out because we don't want to be out here in the dark."

All too familiar feelings began to creep along my spine. I looked nervously into the woods. The trees were thick, blocking out most of the light. "We're going in *there*?" I croaked.

"Yup. You, big fella, head off to my right. And you," he said, eyeing me, "you walk in on my left. Use the sun to navigate."

Sun to navigate? I grew up in Queens, in New York City. Only navigating I could do was hailing a cab.

"Let's go," he barked. I walked so close to him that if I'd gotten any closer he'd be giving me a piggyback ride. "What the . . . ? Spread out. Go to the left! We can't find him all bunched up, and we don't want to be out here when it gets dark."

It took great courage on my part to move into the woods on my own. In less than five minutes the courage ran out. Steve was nowhere in sight. *Well, I'll just head back to the van*, I told myself. I turned around and started walking, but with each step my heart beat a little faster. Nothing looked familiar. Sweat poured down into my eyes. As I caught my breath, my brain whispered two little words that didn't exactly calm me. *You're lost.*

"Help!!!" I screamed. "Joshhhh!!! Crazy driverrrr!!!" Maybe that was a mistake. "Anybody!!! Help!!!"

I heard my echo, then silence. I tried again a few more times before my voice began to give out.

I sat down on a big rock. *Someone will find you*, I

lied to myself. I thought about my parents and my little sister back in Garrettsville. I thought about my friends and wondered what they were up to. Then my thoughts turned to Jessica. Only yesterday I had told her about going away to camp.

"Rodney, why didn't you tell me sooner?" she had asked.

"I didn't know," I explained. "My dopey dad surprised me after the graduation ceremony."

"Well, what about us? What about the lake and the pool and . . ."

"Ugh, I know! I can't get out of it. I've tried. I won't be gone forever."

"How long?"

"Eight weeks."

"Eight weeks? That *is* forever. It's longer. It's the whole summer!"

I tried to calm her. "We'll be going to middle school together in the fall. I'll write you."

"I guess you can always call while you're away, or text . . ."

"Actually, we're not allowed to have cell phones." The words had hung there as she realized we weren't even going to speak. She looked really upset, making my heart sink low into my stomach. It felt the same now, sitting on this rock in the woods.

Sitting on this rock in the woods? I had lost total track of time! It was almost dark now. *Think. What would*

Survival Steve do? Besides killing a moose, he'd probably get something to protect himself. Yes, that's it.

I looked around and found a big stick. I felt better clutching it and headed off in what I hoped was the direction of the van. Just when it was getting so dark I could barely see, I noticed something red up ahead—the baseball cap of the kid who had run off.

"Hey!" I yelled. "Found you!"

He turned around, saw me, and tore off.

"Wait!" I shouted, running after him. There was no way I was going to let this kid leave me alone in the woods. "Stop!" I shouted. The kid looked back, screamed, and kept going. Why was he running away? "Stop running! Get back here," I yelled, my own fear building up again.

After about five minutes of running through thick underbrush and sharp branches—my legs were scratched all over—I noticed a bright glow up ahead. The kid was running toward it. I followed, gaining on him. We were going to be saved!

He bolted through a bush and I dove through too, landing right in the middle of a large crowd of kids, some wearing Camp Wy-Mee T-shirts. The light was from a roaring campfire! I was about to yell, "Thank God, I'm saved," but old Baseball Cap beat me to it.

"Oh, thank God!" he screamed, his voice higher than I expected. "That madman was chasing me through the woods." He pointed at me. "They tried to kill me back at the van!" The kid was gasping for air and looked on the verge of collapse.

My brain reeled with every emotion as I realized I had just gone from saved to public enemy number one. I glanced around at the crowd. No one knew what to make of me as I stood there in my ripped, sweaty, dirty clothes. Their looks ranged from fearful to suspicious to menacing. I glanced at my hand, holding the stick that suddenly resembled a club. "Yikes," I gulped, dropping it with a quick jerk. This was bad. "Wait," I stammered, "it's not what you think . . ."

My mouth, however, couldn't complete the sentence, for at that moment the kid flung off his baseball cap. Long brown hair tumbled down past his shoulders. I mean, *her* shoulders. It was a girl standing there, with emerald green eyes that flashed in the firelight. Even in the middle of the insane moment I could see she was cute. *Real* cute. If I didn't get burned at the stake, summer camp had just gotten a lot more interesting.

Chapter 3

THE FIRE FIGHT

There was a pause as everyone stared at the girl. I guess at first they thought she was a boy, too, but there was no mistaking her now. I started to back away, knowing it was only a matter of seconds before the campfire crowd remembered the madman in their midst.

"This guy tried to kill you?" one boy asked. He was taller than me but looked about my age. Before the girl could answer, he faced the group and ordered, "Grab him!"

Two older teenagers came forward and held me by the arms. The boy giving orders walked up to me as I struggled to break free. Even in the dark I could see he had a white, toothy smile. He flicked his hair to the side like a shampoo model. "Trying to get away?" He laughed. "Not today, weirdo." He gave me a little wink and raised his fist to punch me.

I had never been so scared, which is quite a claim,

considering who I am. Without thinking, though, I lunged forward. The two guys holding my arms banged into the boy, sending him flying backward—right into the fire.

"Oh, Todd!" some girl called out.

Todd screeched, "*Yaaaaaahhhhhhhhhhhooooooooh!*" and jumped up, grabbing his behind.

"The lake!" the girl yelled.

I watched Todd run off into the woods, leaving a smoke trail from his scorched shorts. The guys holding me grabbed even tighter.

I was just starting to ponder my funeral—I pictured Mrs. Lutzkraut smiling happily—when Josh and Survival Steve emerged from the woods. "You got started without me, Rodney!" Josh shouted while grabbing a kid and hurling him over a log. "Fire and fighting. This is awesome. I love camp!"

Survival Steve looked at the guys holding me. "What you fools doin'? Let my passenger be! Josh, settle down."

My captors released me from their grip. At the same moment, Todd returned, his pants dripping wet. He took one look at Survival Steve and sneered. "We got it under control, Mountain Man. You can head back to your shack now."

"What's that, punk?"

"The name's Todd."

"Yeah, I remember you, Turd. Now git!" Steve roared like a grizzly bear and Todd scuttled off into the crowd around the campfire. Next he shouted, "Periwinkle, you down here?"

"Yes," a large tree replied.

Steve glanced about for a second. Not sure where to look, he called out, "These two are with me. I was bringing them in when we had to go in search of another camper."

"Ohhh," the tree answered. Then, slowly, from behind the tree, a head wearing an odd beige pith helmet popped out. Eventually, the rest of the man emerged, and the guy I assumed to be Mr. Periwinkle now stood in the firelight. His outfit matched his helmet. It was all khaki and he looked like an explorer—a skinny, jumpy, nervous explorer.

"Okay then," he finally spoke, eyes darting nervously to make sure the fighting was over. "This looks like a big misunderstanding. Welcome to Camp Wy-Mee! Nice to meet you two, and you, young lady." He waved to the girl.

"She's not with us," Steve pointed out.

"Uh, actually she is," I corrected him. "It's a long story."

Steve glanced at the girl, then at me, then back at the girl. A smile slowly broke across his puzzled face. "Well, I'll be a skinned possum . . ."

"Um, yes, a possum," Mr. Periwinkle continued. "As I was saying, this is the opening night campfire. It's usually a very exciting, fun tradition. Oh, well, I guess it was still exciting. Ha-ha." His laugh sure was nervous. With a strained face, he asked, "Are either of you hurt?" I shook my head and heard him murmur, "Thank God, no lawsuits."

Josh, who had never stopped grinning since he got to camp, explained, "We don't mess around."

"Yes, well, you're quite a strapping fellow," Mr. Periwinkle remarked. "So you're not hurt either, good. No need to call the parents, ha-ha-ha." Again the nervous laugh. "Okay, I guess this is enough campfire for one evening. Counselors, take your campers back to the cabins and prepare for taps. You, douse that fire. And you, move that log . . ."

He continued giving nervous little orders. I was relieved that the threat of violence had passed, at least for now, but this Mr. Periwinkle had said something about calling the parents, and that's exactly what I intended to do first thing in the morning. All I had to do right now was survive the rest of the night.

Chapter 4

A NIGHT AT THE PLAZA

Without the campfire, the air suddenly got colder and the woods grew a lot darker. I looked up through the tall pine trees and noticed a few stars beginning to come out. Mr. Periwinkle was chattering away to the remaining counselors. No one seemed to notice me—except Todd, the kid I had just knocked into the fire. Every few seconds he would shine his flashlight in my eyes to annoy me. It was definitely working.

Turning in my direction, Mr. Periwinkle called over, "You're still standing here?" He said it in a nice enough way.

"I don't know where to go."

"I guess that's a good reason, then." He laughed nervously. "You *did* arrive after the cabin assignments. Let's consult the clipboard." He picked up the board and shuffled through the sheets. "Let me see. Hmmm . . . Rathbone, right?"

"Yes."

"Hmmmm, Rathbone, Rathbone . . . Ah, there we go. Well now, aren't *you* the lucky little camper?"

Was this guy for real? My fellow campers were just about to roast me like a marshmallow. Somehow I didn't feel too lucky.

Periwinkle kept right on beaming. "Yes, you are in for quite a treat. You, my son, have been assigned to the Algonquin cabin."

The name meant little to me. As if reading my mind, he explained that the Algonquins were a Native American tribe. He went on and on about how they carried tomahawks and hunted with bows and arrows in woods just like these. After a minute he stopped midsentence, looking slightly confused. "Where was I? Oh yes, let me find someone to show you the way to the cabin."

As Mr. Periwinkle turned, Todd started in again with the flashlight in my eyes. I was beginning to wish I had a tomahawk of my own when Mr. Periwinkle called out to him. He immediately pointed the light to the ground. "Yes?"

"Please come over here and join us, Todd."

This was the last kid I wanted to give me a welcome tour—or to be my roommate, which was even worse. I had to speak up. "Mr. Periwinkle, isn't there another cabin I could . . ."

"I wouldn't hear of it. Rodney, let me introduce you to Todd Vanderdick. Todd, this is Rodney Rathbone."

The two of us stared at each other, neither one wanting to make the first move. Periwinkle shot nervous glances back and forth between us. His eyes seemed to ask, *Well?* Reluctantly, we shook hands. As they came together, I could feel my skin crawl.

"That's a clammy palm you got there," Todd said, sticking out his big chin.

"Not as clammy as your pants," I answered. "Enjoy the dip in the lake?"

Mr. Periwinkle glanced down. "I say, Todd, what happened to your shorts?"

Todd's eyes narrowed and a sneer curled over his perfect, gleaming teeth. "My hand-tailored $225 Lacoste shorts? I doubt the rodent who ruined them could afford to buy me new ones, but no matter—I have twelve more pairs just like them."

"Excellent," Mr. Periwinkle exclaimed. "It's wise to come prepared. Now, I can see that the two of you are going to be fast friends. Rodney here is in your cabin. I thought you'd like to show him around and introduce him to the boys."

Todd's chin quivered and it looked as though he was trying to eat his own lip. After about ten seconds he became oddly relaxed and his face transformed into an easy smile. The transformation gave me a nervous feeling. With sparkling eyes, he announced, "It would be my pleasure, Mr. Periwinkle."

"Splendid."

Todd held up his finger. "One more thing. What happened to Rodney's big friend?"

"I believe you're referring to young Dumbrowski. He's been assigned to the Cherokee cabin."

"That dump?" Todd laughed.

"Now, Todd, all our facilities here at Camp Wy-Mee can't be . . ."

"Oh, don't get me wrong, Mr. Periwinkle. I think Loserville is the perfect cabin for him, but I'm concerned about Rodney. After all, he'll be *really* far away from his friend. He's going to be all alone. I'll have to take *special* care of him."

"Todd, that's certainly noble of you. You see, Rodney? I leave you in good hands."

Mr. Periwinkle scurried away, and my nerves began firing every warning they knew. I almost collapsed when Todd suddenly gripped my shoulder. "Come on, old sport. Let me show you the way."

I shrugged off his grip as we meandered around trees and bushes. He angled down to a woods path that looked dark and foreboding. I gulped and hesitated. He seemed to sense it and turned back with a smile. "Don't fall behind, Rathbone. This isn't a stroll down Park Avenue. The last thing you want is to wind up lost out here."

He was acting awfully nice . . . for a jerk. Despite my suspicions, I didn't have much choice but to follow him.

★ ★ ★

Moments later we popped out onto a paved path, crossed some playing fields, and walked toward a group of cabins in the distance. I noticed the gleam from a number of flashlights shaking about in the dark. Other campers and counselors were also making the trek, which hopefully meant I wasn't about to get attacked.

"You're going to love the cabin," Todd said. "My dad, Theodore Vanderdick—you know, of *Vanderdick Enterprises*—donated money and his personal architect to spruce up the place."

I had never heard of Vanderdick Enterprises. "Sounds good," I managed.

"Oh, it's a lot better than 'good,' and certainly a lot better than the hole you just crawled out of. Yeah, your luck has turned, hasn't it, chap? Time to see how the other half lives." He spoke to me like I was homeless.

"You know," he continued, "I realize we got off to a bad start, but you have to admit you looked a bit crazy when you first showed up. And besides, now that you're on Team Vanderdick, it's time for a new beginning. What do you say, sport?"

I looked at him. My doubts lingered. He was definitely a stuck-up jerk, but maybe he wasn't out to get me. Maybe he *did* want to be friends. "Well, sorry about knocking you into the fire," I said. "It was an accident." I figured I'd better be nice since I was stuck in his cabin.

"Hey, accidents happen." He held out his hand.

I held out mine, hoping it wasn't clammy, and gave him my best Fred Windbagger handshake.

"That's the spirit," Todd said.

We walked up the path from the fields to a row of cabins. Most of them looked like little huts with some canvas flaps for windows. That is, until we came to a stop in front of one cabin that was three times larger than the rest. It had glass windows, a paved walkway and steps, and what looked like a satellite dish on the roof. I could hear the hum of central air conditioning. "It's not the Plaza, but it's home," Todd said, wiping his feet before pushing open the door.

He was being modest. I didn't think any hotel could be nicer. A group of boys sat around on leather couches, playing a video game on a gigantic flat-screen television that took up the whole wall.

"Hey, fellas, let me introduce to you to Rodney."

They paused the game. Their eyes narrowed and I prayed I wasn't about to get jumped. Some of them probably recognized me from the campfire.

Todd gripped my shoulder. "Rodney is assigned to the Algonquin cabin. Give him a big Team Vanderdick welcome."

The tension left their faces. In unison they chanted, "Bully! Bully! Bully!"

"Where?" I almost screamed, half expecting to see my old enemy, Rocco.

Todd laughed. "Relax, Rathbone. Let me introduce

you to everyone. This is Biff, Skip, Chaz, Blake, Chip"—each gave me a friendly wave—"and over there, that's our counselor, Magnus."

I turned. Standing behind a counter in the kitchen area was a tall, strong-looking blond guy. I figured he was about eighteen. "Velcome. Vat can I fix you to drink?" he asked, shaking a silver cup up and down. "You vant fruit smoothie?"

"Uh, sure."

"Rodney," Todd interrupted, "it looks like your trunk's been dropped off. Maybe you want to put your stuff away. What beds are still available?"

Biff answered, "The Tempur-Pedic and the Euro-Flow 2000 waterbed." He looked kind of sheepish as he added, "The good ones are taken already."

Todd glanced at me. "What do you think?"

"Both sound nice."

"Here's da smoothie," Magnus said, thrusting a cold glass into my hand.

I took a sip and gagged as something slimy slid across the top of my tongue. "Uh, delicious."

"I put in lots of raw egg. Goot for da muscles and da hair." I was fighting the urge to heave and it must have shown. "Vatch da Persian rug!"

Not sure I could survive another sip, I did my best to be polite. "Is that a German accent?" I asked, putting down the smoothie and pushing it a few inches away.

Magnus straightened up to his full height. "I am not

German!" He pounded his chest with his fist. "I am Sveeedish!"

He looked offended, so I said, "I love Sweden!"

"Really?" he asked.

"Oh yeah. Big fan of the meatballs."

"Dere's more to Sveden dan meatballs."

"No doubt," I agreed, struggling hard to think of something else. "Vikings!" I blurted. "I love Vikings."

Magnus smiled and I relaxed—until I noticed his expression start to change. He looked like he was about to cry. "Too bad vee are no longer allowed to raid and pillage. Nothing like dying vit da sword in your hands and going to Valhalla."

"Uh, yeah." The guy was definitely nuts. I looked over to Todd for help.

"Come on, Rodney. I'll show you around the cabin."

We left Magnus in the kitchen—hacking and slicing at the air as if he was raiding a monastery—and toured the rooms. All in all, it was more impressive than I could have imagined. They had every video game system, a pool table, a ping-pong table, a foosball table, and a very nice back deck overlooking the lake.

It was a hundred times better than my house at home!

Slowly, I began to realize that my teacher Mrs. Lutzkraut had gotten me sent to paradise. I wished she could be here to see how her plan had backfired. I was now friends with Josh, this guy Todd seemed okay once you got to know him, and I'd be spending the summer in air-conditioned splendor. I sat down on the couch and folded my hands behind my head. Not bad. Not bad at all.

"There's only one thing we don't have," Todd apologized, "and that's our own bathroom. My dad's lawyers petitioned the head of the local zoning board for a year. When we didn't get our way, Vanderdick Enterprises built a massive prison next to the guy's summerhouse." A big grin spread across Todd's face. "What a loser. You don't mess with Vanderdick Enterprises, right, fellas?" Everyone in the cabin laughed in agreement. "Anyway, long story short, we have to use the boys' division bathroom with all the lowlifes. It's over there."

I looked out through the window. Even in the dark I thought I saw flies buzzing around the building. "Ugh."

Todd nodded. "Be thankful the breeze isn't blowing from the south. Nothing like the scent of old urine to spoil an evening." He stretched and yawned. "It's been a long night. We should turn in. Take the water bed, Rodney. Come on, guys, let's get some shut-eye."

And so for the next twenty minutes I settled in. Following a rather gross visit to the bathroom, I climbed into the water bed. I felt like I was lying on top of the waves. It was fun, and for the first time all day I let myself relax. Just as sleep began to take hold, I remember thinking how lucky I was to be in this cabin with my new friends. Yep, that old witch Lutzkraut had really miscalculated this time.

★ ★ ★

BLAM! BOOM! POP! BANG! I awoke to what sounded like gunfire. I rolled off the wavy bed to the floor and took cover. Yells and screams filled the night. The lights came on and my cabinmates rushed toward the door.

"What is it?"

Biff, who was gazing out the window, yelled, "There's smoke coming from the Loserville cabin!"

We tumbled out into the night. Counselors and campers were running all about. I considered heading back inside for safety but found myself swept along by the crew heading to Loserville.

Magnus boomed, "Voo! Voo!" I thought he'd really lost it until a tall Asian-looking counselor with long black hair stepped out of the smoke. Magnus ran up to him. "Voo, vat is going on?"

"His name is Voo?" I asked Biff, who was standing next to me.

"No, it's Woo."

Before I had a chance to ponder that I moved in closer to hear what Woo had to say.

"The night goes 'Pow!,' man. The campers yell 'Ow!,' man. Everyone's having a cow, man!"

It was confusing, to say the least, but Magnus seemed to understand perfectly. "Zumbody lit firevorks in da cabin!"

"That's certainly what it seems like," said Mr. Periwinkle, walking up to the crowd. I watched him

28

pull his robe around what looked like animal-print pajamas.

"Who vould do dis?" Magnus bellowed, smashing his fist into his palm. "Deese campers could have been hurt."

I looked at the campers who inhabited Loserville. Several of them had smoke-smeared faces and were on the verge of tears. Josh stood off a bit, gazing at the smoke that remained hanging in the air.

"*I* know who did it," Todd suddenly announced. I wasn't expecting this.

"Who?" Magnus and Mr. Periwinkle asked together.

"He's standing right there."

I leaned my head in to see the culprit. What happened next was a complete shock. Todd pointed straight at me. "I'm very disappointed in you, Rathbone, though I can't say I'm surprised, given your upbringing."

"Huh?" I managed. Suddenly a sinking, sad feeling hit me in the gut as I realized what was about to happen. How could I have been so stupid? I had let myself believe that Todd really wanted to be my friend.

"I found these in Rodney's trunk," he lied, holding up several packs of fireworks. "His trunk was left open and I just happened to notice them. There's more where these came from."

"But I don't have any fireworks," I stammered. "I was asleep the whole night."

"Sure, Rathbone," he continued, "that's why I saw

29

you sneaking back from Loserville." His lips curled into a villainous leer and he gave me a subtle wink. No one else seemed to notice it, but I knew my excellent new buddy Todd had just framed me.

"Let's go and look in his trunk!" Magnus barked.

Todd wasn't finished. He grabbed the counselor's elbow. "Oh, we will, Magnus, but before I show you the proof of Rodney's guilt, I think we need to check on tonight's poor victims."

Where was he going with all this? I looked around at the crowd. Everyone was giving me nasty looks. Even Mr. Periwinkle seemed annoyed.

Todd walked over to the whimpering Loserville campers. "Are you guys okay?" he asked, giving one young boy a brotherly pat on the shoulder.

Mr. Periwinkle said, "You're right, Todd. I admire your compassion. We need to look into their well-being before we deal with Rodney."

Todd brought his hands to his heart. While he tried to look sincere, I caught a gleam in his eye that told me he wasn't finished plotting my doom. He walked up to Josh. "And how do you feel?"

"Hungry," Josh answered.

"I mean, how do you feel that your friend Rodney set off all these explosives in your cabin and that some-one—even you—might have gotten hurt?"

This time Josh gave it some thought. "Still hungry."

I got ready to make a run back into the woods. Todd

was trying to get Josh to attack me. That was his plan!

Todd continued, "Can you believe Rodney would set off fires right next to where you were sleeping? What are you going to do about that?"

"Rodney," Josh barked, "*you* lit that fire?"

"Uhhh," was all I could manage, for even as I tried to think of something to say, Josh was already running at me. I tried to back away, but Magnus seemed to be blocking any escape.

Josh reached me, and I cringed in expectation of the pain. Instead of punching me, though, he put me in a big bear hug. He was going to crush me. What a way to die!

"That was the best, Rodney!" he yelled.

"Huh?" Todd and I said together.

"You knew I love fires! And you made big, banging fires! It's the nicest thing anyone's ever done for me!"

"Ah, well, I thought you'd like it," I said, making sure no one else could hear.

I had never seen Josh so happy. The same couldn't be said for the others—especially Todd, who knew not to push his luck with Josh by my side. I watched as he turned and stormed off with Magnus and the other Algonquins. Mr. Periwinkle shuffled over to us.

"My, my, you two haven't been in camp for one full evening and already all heck's broke loose."

He looked upset and I felt bad for him. "Mr. Periwinkle . . . ," I started to explain.

"It's no good, Rodney. Guess there isn't much use

trying to sleep now. I'll meet you in my office once I get everything here settled."

He walked off into the crowd of campers. So much had happened that I could barely make sense of it all. Josh, on the other hand, had no such problem. He was still grinning away like a kid at a birthday party.

At least someone had enjoyed the first night of camp.

Chapter 5

A SECOND CHANCE

I had been escorted to a camp office on the lower level of Mr. Periwinkle's house. Now, as I waited for him, I watched the blackness outside slowly turn gray. Dawn couldn't be far off. I heard a slight nervous cough, followed by Mr. Periwinkle's voice as he entered the room and sat down behind a big wooden desk.

You'd think I'd be nervous, but there was nothing intimidating about Mr. Periwinkle. Besides, I expected to get kicked out and that's exactly what I wanted. I'd had enough of this crazy Camp Wy-Mee and all the horrible people in it. The farther away from Todd Vanderdick, the better. For the first time in my life, I actually looked forward to receiving my punishment.

"Well, Rodney, that was quite an evening you put us through," Mr. Periwinkle began.

"I didn't light the fireworks."

"Um, well, there was a good bit of evidence in your trunk that says otherwise."

"Todd put it there, and he lit it. How else would he have known to look in the trunk?"

"He claims to have seen it when you opened it to get your toothbrush, and we need to remember, Todd is a Vanderdick."

"I'll say."

"His father is a pillar of the community, and young Todd has won the Camp Wy-Mee Leadership Award the past two summers."

"Well, his plot to frame me did show outstanding initiative."

"It certainly did," he agreed. Then his face grew confused. "Oh, now, now, I think we need to dismiss the conspiracy theories. What we need—"

"Listen, Mr. Periwinkle, I don't care. Kick me out of this asylum."

He looked taken aback. He paused and stared down. His hands rested next to a paperweight and a mug full of pens and markers. "It pains me," he continued, "to hear a camper describe Camp Wy-Mee as an asylum. I think if you were to stay with us for the summer, Rodney, you would discover that this is a magical place. But, sadly, you've left me little choice. I'm going to have to call your parents to come get you." He reached for the phone.

"Per-CY!"

Mr. Periwinkle jumped, knocking over the mug of pens. "Oh dear," he stammered, looking up at the ceiling. "Coming, sweetie!"

He took off through the office door. I heard him move through the house and up the stairs. I strained my ears to hear the conversation in the room above me. It was too muffled for me to make out the words, but I could tell that whoever had called Mr. Periwinkle was a woman with a sharp, bossy voice.

After a minute I heard Mr. Periwinkle retrace his path back to the office. He looked red and more flustered than usual. He sat back down and ran his hands over his face. He exhaled and said, "Well, Rodney, it seems that Mrs. Periwinkle thinks you deserve a second chance. You've been forgiven."

"What? Why?" I stammered.

"I don't really know. In over thirty years of marriage she's never given *me* a second chance."

"So I'm not being punished?"

"Oh, I didn't say that. No, she wants you punished severely. Just not sent home."

"But I don't want to stay here. I want to speak to my parents."

"She said no phone calls."

Something seemed fishy, but I didn't care. I had no intention of sticking around to discover what these people were up to. "I'm calling home," I said, reaching over for the phone. I punched in my phone number.

"Oh dear," Mr. Periwinkle whined, biting his nails. "Oh, don't do that. You should hang up." He glanced nervously back at the ceiling.

"Hello," came my dad's sleepy voice through the receiver.

"DAD!" I yelled.

"Rodney! What is it? Why are you calling so early? Honey, Rodney's on the phone." I could hear my mom talking in the background.

"Dad, you've got to come up here and get me. Everyone here is mean. This kid framed me, said I set off some fireworks, now the camp director says I'm going to be punished severely."

"What?" my dad barked. "I didn't pay all that money to send you off somewhere to be picked on and punished. I'll have you out of there before dark! Is the camp director near?"

"Yes, he's sitting right here." Mr. Periwinkle jumped back.

"Let me talk to him."

I handed the phone over. Mr. Periwinkle held the receiver to his ear, reluctantly, as if it might bite him.

I felt great. My dad was going to get me out of here. I watched and listened as Mr. Periwinkle cleared his throat and began stammering.

"Yes . . . yes, well we did find some in his trunk and . . . well, we've decided to give him another chance. . . . There needs to be some punishment. . . . Oh, well that's too bad . . . I'm sure he'd learn to love the place. . . . What's that? . . . No, there are no refunds. . . . No, it's stated right there in the contract. . . . Yes, we have to be quite firm about the *no-refund policy*." Mr. Periwinkle listened for a moment more. "Okay, I'll give it to him." He handed me the phone.

"Rodney," my dad said, "I've given it some thought, and I've decided I didn't raise you to be a quitter."

"Dad, you just said . . ."

"Rodney. You're a Rathbone. Time to give it the old college try."

"But I'm just starting middle school!"

"Well, that's beside the point. Anyway, you need to give that camp another shot. There are no two ways about it. I know you can handle everyone there. Look what you did this past year at school. If you don't like it in a couple of weeks, call me again."

"But, Dad . . ."

"Rodney, I love you. Talk to you soon. I have to get ready for work. Have fun." *Click*. I felt my heart drop into my stomach.

Mr. Periwinkle clapped his hands together. "Well, now, that's settled. Okay, we need to get ready for breakfast . . ."

A sharp tap at the partially open window interrupted his sentence. Todd's toothy grin appeared on the other side of the screen. "I brought Rodney's things," he called into the room. I wanted to hurl the paperweight in his direction.

"Excellent, Todd," Mr. Periwinkle said.

Todd gave me one of his evil smiles. "Rodney, you're going to need to get your trunk latch fixed. Darn thing sprung open on me." I craned my neck and saw my belongings lying all over the grass.

Mr. Periwinkle spoke up. "Todd, it turns out that Rodney is going to remain with us for a while. So we'll need to get his stuff back to the cabin."

Todd frowned. "I think that's a bad idea." He paused, expecting Mr. Periwinkle to change his mind. When no reply came, he added, "Well, he's not staying in *my* cabin. My parents always say that it's important for me to associate with 'the right sort.' I don't think an arsonist is right-sort material."

"Hmmm. I guess I could change his cabin . . ."

"Put him in Loserville," Todd suggested.

"Its proper name is Cherokee," Mr. Periwinkle corrected him.

"Yeah, whatever. It would be a good way to start the healing process."

"Yes . . . so it would be. Wonderful idea!" Mr. Periwinkle turned around to face me. "Isn't Todd thoughtful?"

That wasn't exactly the word I had in mind. Todd was punching his fist into his palm and making faces at me behind Periwinkle's back.

"Now, why don't you gather your things?" suggested Mr. Periwinkle. "The cabins will be coming to line up for breakfast shortly."

Todd shouted into the office, "See you later, Mr. Periwinkle. I've got to go make my bed, wash my hands before breakfast, and see if any new kids need help finding their way around."

I wanted to puke, but Periwinkle seemed to really believe him.

"Wonderful. Thank you, Todd. You know, Rodney, you could learn a thing or two from this one. You can see why I couldn't take your framing story seriously."

I didn't answer. I may have been in a new location, but my life sure hadn't changed. I had a bully after me, no one believed what I had to say, and it looked like I might be stuck here for a long, long time.

Chapter 6

HOME, STRANGE HOME

There were about a dozen cabins in the boys' area, but I had no problem spotting Loserville. Even if I hadn't seen it during the night, you couldn't miss it by day. The cabin was sagging in the middle—but that was nothing compared to the weeds growing on the roof and the tattered canvas windows. The fact that some kid had scrawled the word "Loserville" across the front door also made it kind of easy to spot. Either way, there was no mistaking it for the Algonquin cabin.

"Catching a ray or sliding away?"

I spun around. The counselor, Woo, had walked up in back of me. He was holding a towel and probably heading back from the bathroom.

"What?" I asked.

He wore glasses with big black frames and had a black cap thing that looked like a flying saucer on his head. Later I found out he called it a beret, and the little beard on his chin was called a goatee. "Hand me that skin, daddy-o," he said, sticking out his hand. "I'm Woo, and I know what to do."

"Nice to meet you. I'm Rodney."

His head started bopping back and forth as he said, "Rod*ney*, swings from the *tree*, drinks some *tea*, gots to go *pee*." I wasn't sure if he was singing, rapping, or just having a fit. "Play sax, daddy-o?" he asked.

"Excuse me?"

"You on the stick?"

"Huh?"

"Saxophone, *man*. I need a tenor saxophone for my jazz ensemble. We play a lot of Miles Davis. I play the trumpet, the straw boss. Dig?"

I still wasn't following. "No, I don't play saxophone."

His face fell, but then brightened as he asked, "What about the bass guitar? Bum bum bum bum . . ." He stood there looking down at me making the bum-bum noise and plucking an imaginary guitar in the air.

"No," I said, "I don't play the guitar. Actually, the reason I'm here is because I was just assigned to your cabin."

A big grin spread across his face. "Well, come feel the funk and grab a bunk!"

I found myself smiling, too—for the first time since arriving at Camp Wy-Mee. This Woo guy was crazy but nice. He reached down, picked up my trunk, and announced, "Follow me, man, to Cherokee land."

And follow him I did, though I couldn't help

wondering how my new cabinmates would react to me. After all, in their eyes I was the guy who had attacked them during the night. I doubted I'd be welcomed with open arms, especially since the smell of fireworks still hung in the air.

Once inside the cabin, I noticed several kids huddled about and whispering. Others were staring off into space. Josh sat cross-legged on a top bunk, picking at his toenails. He gave me a nod. "Yo! Rodney."

"Yo," I answered back.

Still in shock—but grateful—that Josh was my new best buddy, I looked around, unsure of what to do. I figured I better claim a bunk. Sleeping bags lay on all except two of them. One of the available bunks was right below Josh, but as I approached I saw that his mattress sagged all the way down in the middle. The idea of rusty old springs an inch from my face didn't exactly excite me. The other available bunk contained a nasty-looking gray pillow. I went to move it.

Snap!

The pillow almost bit my finger off! I jumped back and watched it rise on four legs and hiss at me. It was a raccoon.

"You don't want to wake up Harry," some kid said.

"Is he like a pet?" I asked.

"No. He's far from tame. He just moved in here last summer and no one can get him out. Did you get your rabies shots?"

All at once those straining, rusty springs below Josh didn't seem so bad. I put my trunk next to the empty bottom mattress, sat down, and checked out my new surroundings.

There was no denying that my cabinmates were a pretty motley-looking group. Several of them still wore the smoke stains and dirt of the night before, leading me to believe that hygiene wasn't a priority in this cabin. My feeling was reinforced when I noticed another boy with sweaty armpits that had soaked through his T-shirt. He was busy picking something out of his ear. The next kid was clean, but perhaps even more disturbing. He wore a sky-blue dunce cap and matching cape. I guessed he was going for the wizard look.

Now, I've always prided myself on not being judg-mental, but I was beginning to wonder if I had more in common with the raccoon than the rest of this Los-erville gang. Just then the door opened and another boy stepped in. He was thin, with dark, tanned skin and brown, almost black eyes. His black hair was combed neatly back, and what was even more shock-ing was that he was confident and cool. Maybe he had wandered in by accident, because he sure looked out of place.

He must have been thinking the same about me. "You look halfway normal," he announced. "A relief. I'm Fernando. Who are you?"

"Rodney."

"Sure, the terrorist trainee. We know all about you."

Here we go, I started to think. Woo was on the far side of the cabin, eyes closed, tapping his foot and listening to his iPod. He wouldn't be any help. I stared back at the kid, ready for a fight—until I noticed he was grinning slightly.

"You know, Rodney, the Fourth of July isn't until next week."

"Hey, I didn't light the fire crack—"

Fernando interrupted. "Do you know that this bunch"—he motioned around the cabin—"has been whimpering for hours? Well, not that big fellow up there, he seemed to enjoy the whole show, but the explosions got Stinky sweating, and that's not fun, I assure you."

I assumed he was talking about the armpits kid. "Listen," I said, holding up my hand, "I didn't . . ."

"You didn't do it." Fernando laughed. "We know."

I thought he was being sarcastic. "I'm serious. I didn't . . ."

Fernando rubbed his temples. "You're not one of those guys that needs everything repeated five times, are you? We know you didn't do it."

"You do? How?"

"Because we know who did it. Thorin Oakenshield over here"—he thumbed back at Wizard Boy—"saw Todd Vanderdick last night."

Thorin Oak-and-something stepped forward. "I saw

44

him sneak into our cabin. I was ready to grab him, but he must have hit me with an Immobulus spell, because I couldn't move or speak."

"Yeah, that's called being too scared to move," Stinky joked.

"Scared?" Thorin snapped. "I happen to be the most important dwarf in Middle Earth!"

"Last year you were Aslan, King of Narnia, which is ridiculous since Aslan is a lion."

"Ridiculous? ROOOAARRRR!" He jumped across the cabin with his hands held out like cat claws. Stinky countered by ripping off his dingy sneaker and holding it in the air. Thorin gagged and fell away holding his nose. "Not foot odor! It's my greatest weakness!"

The two of them broke into hee-hawing laughs.

"Do you see what I have to put up with?" Fernando asked me. "Welcome to Loserville." He held out his hand. I shook it and knew right away that here was a kid I liked.

"And my name is Frank," Stinky added.

Each kid in the cabin came up and said hello to me. Even if they were a bit odd, I could see that they were genuinely nice. I relaxed and yawned. I hadn't exactly had a good night's sleep. I closed my eyes for a minute, thinking about what Todd had done to me. I sure was glad to be away from him and the other Algonquin phonies. Maybe there were no flat-screen

TVs or water beds here, but hey, my new friends seemed great, and besides, we had something you'd never find in the Algonquin cabin. I smiled as Harry the Raccoon waddled across the floor and disappeared below a bunk.

Chapter 7

LUCIFER

"Snake 'em, break 'em, and shake 'em!"

I jumped. Woo was yelling from outside the cabin. I must have fallen asleep for a minute. "What did he just say?" I asked Stinky.

"That it's time to line up for breakfast and that we're having scrambled eggs today."

"Oh." Completely confused, I followed the rest of the campers outside, where they were gathering before heading to the dining hall. By now the sun was really up and I took a few moments to take in my surroundings.

The cabins overlooked a very large lake. In the distance, beautiful green islands—some of them pretty big—dotted the surface of the deep blue water. There were canoes, rowboats, kayaks, sailboats, a dock, and swim platforms. Closer, in a clearing, were basketball courts and several poles, each with a yellowish ball hanging down from the top. Already boys were whacking the balls in opposite directions.

"What game is that?" I asked Thorin.

"Tetherball. Not exactly Dungeons and Dragons, if you ask me."

"Of course," I answered, not sure what to say.

Looking in the other direction, heading away from the lake, there was a path that eventually opened up to the large fields I had crossed during the night. I could see soccer goals and a volleyball court. I hated to admit it, but by daylight the place looked awesome. Every direction held interesting things to do. "Seems pretty nice," I mentioned to Josh.

"I guess," he answered. "Got more fireworks?"

I changed the subject. "Looks like we'll be eating soon."

"I know. Bet they'll have food."

In search of more interesting conversation, I strolled over to Fernando. "So," I began, "do you mind if I ask—how did you wind up in Loserville?"

"Same as you."

He motioned straight ahead. Todd was standing outside the Algonquin cabin talking to Magnus. He must have noticed us because he immediately pulled up his shorts as high as they'd go, stuck out his front teeth, and walked around like a nerd with mental problems. "Uh duhhh, losers!" he yelled and waved. The other Algonquins laughed, and I noticed Stinky cowering. Fernando, on the other hand, remained completely cool.

"You see," he continued, "the ladies love me, and ol' Todd over there doesn't like that, so he had me assigned here. I don't really blame him. Being as smooth and charming as Fernando is intimidating." He laughed and I joined him. "And speaking of the ladies," he turned to me, "I understand you arrived with quite a beauty last night."

I thought about the girl with the emerald-green eyes I had chased through the woods, straight to the campfire. Remembering just how good she looked, my chest pounded. I had trouble inhaling as I thought of her long brown hair. But I was supposed to be going out with Jessica. And yet . . .

"Are you okay, my friend?" Fernando asked. "We lost you for a minute."

"Oh. Um, what were we talking about?"

"Never mind for now." His gaze had returned to Todd. "I have to warn you, Rodney. If I were you, I would watch my back. That Vanderdick kid is a total—"

BLLLEEEEHHHHHH, a whistle blasted.

"Line up by cabins!" Magnus yelled. "Time vee go now to da flag raising und breakfast!"

As we marched off toward a big building that I guessed was the dining hall, some other counselors started a song about sixpence, a whiskey bottle, and an unhappy wife. Many of the campers joined in. I didn't know the words but it was kind of fun striding along with Fernando, Stinky, Josh, and Thorin Oakenshield.

The sweet smell of grass filled my nostrils, and though early in the day, the summer heat was already baking the blacktop.

Despite my Todd problems—and the fact that I wanted to get back to my friends in Garrettsville as soon as possible—I could see that Camp Wy-Mee wasn't a complete disaster.

And then I saw something that made me feel even better. The girls were heading our way! There were a lot of them, and they were also singing. I strained to see one in particular. A moment later our eyes met and my knees almost gave out. In the light of day, not covered in dirt and grime, the girl I had chased to the campfire looked even better. I saw her returning my look. A friend of hers whispered something in her ear and she looked at me with greater intensity. I could feel my pulse quickening as we came to a stop.

Magnus hollered, "Campers, straighten out da lines and stop da talking! Vee vill now listen to Mr. Perivinkle, ya?"

Dressed in safari attire, Mr. Periwinkle stood on a hill to the right of the dining hall. "Okay, okay, everyone. We all need to be quiet for the flag raising. You down there"—he pointed to Thorin Oakenshield—"please remove your, er, hat. Thank you. Now for the part I know you've been waiting for all year." The crowd shifted its attention to the Periwinkle house, adjacent to the hill. The house had nice views and big old trees surrounding it. Unfortunately, my earlier visit to the camp office inside had tarnished my feelings. Mr. Periwinkle called, "Sweetie! We're ready!"

Out from behind the house appeared a large, stern woman on a horse. She sat there for a moment looking down at us, and I assumed she was the one I had heard screeching at Mr. Periwinkle last night. What came out of her mouth next sounded even more frightening.

"Oh say, can you seeeeeee . . ."

Her voice was cutting and awful and sliced right through the air. It seemed to take forever to raise the flag and I said a silent prayer of thanks when the song ended. "Is that Periwinkle's wife?" I asked Thorin.

"Yes. She rides around on that old steed as if it were Shadowfax . . ."

"Silence!" Mrs. Periwinkle shouted in our direction. Then, to her husband, she announced, "Percy, I am ready to survey the troops! I mean, campers."

She trotted down the hill on her horse, with Mr. Periwinkle running alongside. When she reached the crowd of campers, she began to ride more slowly and deliberately, looking down at each group. She wore a silver riding helmet and I felt a natural urge to stick out my chest and salute.

We were the last group to be inspected. As Mrs. Periwinkle passed by, her horse turned its head, took a step in my direction, and looked down into my eyes. It was so close I could feel the hot breath from its nostrils on my face. I didn't know what to do. Finally I said, "Hey, boy," and reached out my hand to . . .

"Neeeeigh!!" Immediately, the horse reared up and tried to bring down its front hooves on top of me. I had to dive backward and actually fell into a little ditch. As I tumbled down I heard the horse's whinnies and the shrieks of Mrs. Periwinkle, combined with a kid's voice yelling, "Whoa! Whoa!"

I came to a stop in a clump of overgrown grass. Only after I was sure the horse was subdued did I climb back up, expecting to be swarmed by concerned people. Boy, was I wrong. Mrs. Periwinkle was off the horse, helmet tilted on the side of her head. Her clothes looked disheveled. I wondered if she'd been thrown. She looked a bit like a teapot about to boil over. As Mr. Periwinkle fanned her face, she pointed a finger at me and barked, "*Who* is this ruffian?"

Mr. Periwinkle bobbed up and down several times nervously, unable to speak. It was Todd who answered. He was holding the horse by its reins and patting it like an old friend.

"That," he told Mrs. Periwinkle, "is Rodney Rathbone . . . the one who caused all the commotion last night."

She pursed her lips. "I knew it was a risk keeping this deviant about. My poor Lucifer could have been badly hurt . . . "

This was too much. "I didn't do anything to your horse," I explained.

"Silence! You are a menace. Percy!"

"Yes, dear?"

"I want this boy soundly punished for last night, and for today. Just look at my blouse."

"It looks . . . lovely," Mr. Periwinkle lied. I cringed. He continued, "How about I have Rodney here assist Gertrude and Alice with kitchen cleanup for a week?"

Mrs. Periwinkle looked at her husband. "That's a start, but I don't think it's going to be enough. First we'll suspend all his phone privileges."

"What?" I yelled. I couldn't lose my calls. I was already planning to get my dad back on the phone later that day.

Now it was Todd's turn to join the conversation. "You heard her, Rathbone." He was acting like their long-lost son, and I didn't like it. He continued, "You know, Mrs. Perwinkle, the other day, when Dad and I were standing on your schooner's poop deck . . ."

"Ha ha, he said *poop*!" Josh laughed.

Everyone glared at him, but clearly he didn't understand the meaning of eye contact and continued laughing for a bit. Mrs. Periwinkle shook her head in disgust before turning back to Todd. "You were saying?"

"Well, when Dad and I were so graciously invited on your boat, I noticed that the bottom of the schooner hadn't been cleaned in years. It's covered with zebra mussels. Have you heard of zebra mussels? They're nasty creatures with sharp shells." He looked at me with a sideways glance before continuing. "I think Rodney here should have to remove them."

"Yes," Mrs. Periwinkle replied, "that's an excellent idea, Todd. I'll have him remove them. I like that." As she pondered my punishment, she seemed momentarily calm and happy.

"Excuse me, but isn't the boat in the water?" I asked.

"Duhhhh . . . it's a boat," Todd shot back. "Of course it's in the water."

"How will I get at the bottom, then?"

Mrs. Periwinkle answered this time. "You'll swim!" Her eyes locked onto mine. Her face twisted in a sly smile, and for a dreadful second I noticed a sinister flash. A flash that, while it seemed impossible, I knew I'd seen before. I shivered.

"Enough talk!" she commanded. "Mr. Periwinkle will arrange the particulars." She took one final look at me and my cabinmates. "Now, go to breakfast, and take your greasy little friends with you!"

Chapter 8

ROUGH SAILING

The next few days consisted of basic camp orientation. We went over safety procedures and rules, and learned where everything was. It had started raining on my second night at Camp Wy-Mee and continued to pour nonstop, which gave me plenty of time to get to know my "greasy" friends. They were great and we had lots of fun playing cards in the cabin, careful to dodge the raindrops coming down from the leaky roof. Woo would play jazz trumpet in the corner, and sometimes we would all just goof around for hours at a time.

It would have been awesome, actually, except that Todd had it in for me and I was forced to spend most of my time avoiding him. Worst of all, every day I was stuck washing pots and pans in the dining hall. It got to the point where it was too much. I just wanted to go home. I liked my new friends, but I missed Rishi,

Slim, and the gang I had left behind. I missed Jessica, too. Heck, I even missed my little sister.

The worst part was that I couldn't even call my family. Mrs. Periwinkle had made sure of that when she suspended my phone privileges. I figured that some of the kids had snuck in cell phones, but everyone told me it didn't matter. Evidently, Camp Wy-Mee was the only place left on Earth without cell reception!

After each meal, with my hands stuck in hot, greasy water, I would dream of ways to escape this prison. At least the lunch ladies, Alice and Gertrude, were kind. From time to time they would wave their spatulas at me and flash toothless smiles through clouds of cigarette smoke.

It was on my last day of kitchen duty that the sun finally came out. I worked extra fast, dried off the final pots and pans, and bolted out of the hot kitchen—right into Mr. Periwinkle.

"Ah, Rodney, did you find any classes you're excited about?"

"Huh?"

"Now that the rain has stopped we can truly get going with camp."

He motioned around and I realized that tables had been arranged in the field. Campers were wandering between them, checking out the different classes being offered. I looked at Mr. Periwinkle. "Got anything on how to remove burned-on grease from soaking pans?"

"Ah, yes, that was an excellent lesson. We're all about building character at Camp Wy-Mee."

"Yeah, great. Mr. Periwinkle, can't I use the phone? It's been a week. I need to call my parents."

His face lost some of its excitement. "Rodney, if your parents wanted to talk to you, would they have sent you away to camp?"

That gave me pause. Could it be true? I shook the thought out of my head. "But . . ."

"You can write them a letter tonight. Now go out there to the field and find some nice activities . . ."

"Mr. Periwinkle, I'm not planning on staying here, so there's no need for me to pick any activities. I've had enough character building for one lifetime and I really need to call—"

"Ah, here's someone you could learn a thing or two from!"

I turned around. Josh was walking by with a big smile on his face. "Rodney, I got into riflery, archery, and rocketry. I get to shoot guns and arrows, and explode rockets! I can't wait. This place is the greatest!" He ran off with his hands raised in the air.

We watched him go. Turning back to Mr. Periwinkle, I noticed his eyes looked wet. He shook his head and said wistfully, "If I had twenty more like him, I'd have the top camp in America."

After digesting Periwinkle's drivel and realizing I wasn't going to get any further with him, I headed out into the field. I wasn't excited about looking for classes, but I figured I'd better do it. After all, it was starting to dawn on me that escape from Camp Wy-Mee might be harder than I thought. Just then I saw Fernando. "Pick any classes?" I asked.

"Not yet. It's important to know which classes they're registering for first." He seemed to be looking for someone.

"Who's registering for?" I asked.

He glanced at me with a puzzled expression, and then gazed back into the crowd. I could see his eyes darting from one girl to the next. He nodded and counted to himself as they signed up for classes. Eventually he pointed to a red-haired girl and raised his eyebrows. "That's the one for Fernando. How about you, Rodney? Whose class are you joining?"

I hadn't thought about picking classes based on which girls were in them, but at that moment Emerald Eyes walked by. She was wearing a white headband and giggling with a friend. I nodded toward her dumbly. Fernando approved. "Yes, I should have guessed. You have excellent taste."

"Yeah, well, she hates me. I've tried twice this week to talk to her and she's always walked right by. She still thinks of me as the crazy kid who chased her through the woods."

"That's wonderful news."

"Huh?"

"Don't you see?" He smiled. "The fact that she hates you will make the quest that much more interesting."

I could tell he wasn't kidding, but I also knew it didn't matter. No quests for this camper. I was dating Jessica . . . I hoped. "I have a girlfriend," I told him.

"That's nice, I have six. Now, see that one over there? I'll bet she'll love it when I speak to her in my Latin tongue."

Not quite sure what that meant or what to expect, I watched as he headed off in the direction of the red-headed girl. She turned around, looking confused, but then her eyes started to twinkle and she smiled. "Is that Spanish?" she asked. Fernando looked back at me and winked.

I laughed and started to turn away, then stopped. The girl with the green eyes had entered a building down by the lake. I noticed the sign above it: EXPERT SAILING CLASS.

Figuring I had nothing to lose, I decided to follow her in, when a little voice inside my head reminded me that I didn't know the first thing about sailing. Heck, the only boat I'd ever been on was the Staten Island Ferry!

"Who cares?" I said out loud.

Several people turned and looked at me. Woo was walking by and whispered, "Crazy like a crazy man. Cut the gas. Dig?"

I didn't dig, and I didn't care. Maybe crazy was the thing to be at this point. I walked right over to expert sailing and entered. The girl who had kept me captivated since arriving at camp was sitting alone on a bench. She looked up and my heart jumped into my throat. I wished I knew Spanish. "Hey, I'm Rodney."

"I know who you are. We kind of met already, remember?"

I couldn't believe I was finally talking to her. "Uh, yeah, about that, I wasn't trying to attack you. I was actually trying to help, but I think I, well, what I really meant to do was try and, well, if you want to know the truth, I really was planning on . . ."

She laughed. "Relax. I realize now you're not a killer. I'm Tabitha, by the way. You're signing up for this class?" She waved her hand behind her. I eyed the sails, ropes, and other widgets and gadgets that I knew nothing about. On the chalkboard was a list of unfamiliar words. Maybe I should rethink the expert sailing thing.

"Well . . ."

She interrupted. "I love sailing and sailors. I think there's nothing more amazing than an experienced sailor at the helm of a boat. The sea is so romantic. The waves and wind, it's like nothing else." Her bright eyes looked deeply into mine. "You must be quite a sailor to sign up for this class."

"You have no idea."

"I guess we'll be sailing together, then. You know, the end-of-summer sailing regatta at my father's club is probably the highlight of my year."

"Yes, same at my father's club," I lied. The only club my dad belonged to was Costco.

"I just love to be in a boat with people who really know what they're doing," she continued.

I was getting so carried away that I couldn't stop myself. "Me too. In fact, I was the New York junior yachting champ three years in a row."

Before she had a chance to answer, someone walked in carrying a box that blocked his face. "Tabitha," I heard him say, "I'm so glad you're signing up for the class. The two of us are going to have some awesome sails together this summer." I couldn't see who it was but the voice had already become nauseatingly familiar. He set the box down and noticed me. "It's you! Why don't you go slither back under whatever rock you crawled out from?"

"Nice to see you, too, Todd."

"You're an expert sailor? Look at what you're wearing. You've got to be kidding me!"

I looked down at the New York Knicks jersey I had gotten for my birthday. Then I glanced at his attire. He wore a yellow button-down shirt and baby-blue shorts with pink sailboats on them.

"I'm sorry," I told him, "I didn't know I was supposed to borrow my mother's clothes for this class."

Tabitha giggled and Todd slammed down the box he was holding. He removed his expensive-looking sunglasses and took a step in my direction. This was it.

"Ah, my expert sailors," Mr. Periwinkle greeted us. I hadn't noticed him enter the room but was sure glad to see him. "Rodney, I knew you'd find something you liked. Oh, and Todd, can I borrow you for half an hour? You other two . . . no need to hang around here. I'm sure there are other classes to explore."

As Tabitha and I got up to leave, Todd whispered, "That's the last time I take an insult from you, Rathbone. Next time you won't be so lucky."

I understood all too well that his anger went beyond me. Good ol' Todd wanted Tabitha all to himself—and here I was, walking out the door with her into the beautiful sunshine.

Chapter 9

ADIOS, AMIGOS

Mr. Periwinkle found me the next afternoon as I hid—I mean, rested—under a big old beech tree overlooking the great field. I was trying to avoid Todd and the other Algonquin goons.

"Ah, Rodney, fancy meeting you here. This is a most inspiring spot. You know, I climbed this beech tree when I was a boy."

"You went to camp here?" I asked. Suddenly I pictured him at my age, climbing the beautiful tree. Its smooth branches angled everywhere. It was the best climbing tree I'd ever seen.

"Yes, Rodney. I came to Camp Wy-Mee one summer many years ago and have never really left it." The leaves rustled softly in the breeze, and I took a moment to read the various names and dates carved into the thick gray trunk over the years. "Right up there. Read that one," Mr. Periwinkle suggested.

I couldn't miss it. PERCY + HAGATHA 4 EVER.

"*Hagatha?*" I asked.

"That's Mrs. Periwinkle to you." He smiled. "I met her at age seventeen when I was a counselor here. Her family owned the camp even then." He turned and his eyes glazed over as he looked out at the fields. We could see paths heading off to the many different camp destinations. In the distance, the forest looked dense and wild. A dragonfly, buzzing like a B-17, flew right past us, breaking Periwinkle's trance.

"Rodney, there are a few things to go over. Mrs. Periwinkle hasn't forgotten about that zebra mussel punishment Todd suggested, and now that the weather is nice, I suggest you get to it. I have a paint scraper, snorkel gear, and some buckets waiting . . ."

"Wait, you want me to *collect* the mussels?"

"You bet. It'll save us a fortune." He smiled and rubbed his palms together.

"What?" I yelled.

"Never mind that. I have other news. It seems that we will be unable to offer expert sailing this summer."

Secretly relieved, I asked, "Why not?"

"Too few campers signed up for it. And besides, the insurance premiums are through the roof this year. Anyway, I've moved you, Todd, and that girl into athletics class with Mr. Cramps."

I'd heard that was a class to avoid. "Do you have any *more* good news for me?"

Missing my sarcasm, he replied, "Sadly, that's it for now, but just think—athletics class, a nice little cooling swim this afternoon . . . the world is your clam."

He turned toward his house to leave. "Jeepers!" he gasped. Panic wiped away his usual smile as his face turned pale. "Oh dear. I didn't think it would actually happen."

I spun around. Pulling up in front of the Periwinkle house was a large, black Mercedes followed by an SUV. Three men in dark suits and mirrored sunglasses climbed out of the Mercedes, and walked towards the front porch. Each carried a briefcase. We watched the front door swing open. Mrs. Periwinkle stepped outside and greeted them.

"Oh gosh golly . . . I'd better be off. Have a nice swim, Rodney."

Instead of heading home, though, he slunk into the bushes and disappeared. I looked back one last time in the direction of his house, trying to figure out what had made Mr. Periwinkle turn white and act so strange. It was then that I noticed the sign on the passenger side of the SUV. VANDERDICK ENTERPRISES.

I spent the whole afternoon in murky, slimy water, scraping the schooner clean and collecting Periwinkle's mussels. I was furious—and starving—by the time I reached the dining hall for dinner. Eventually, I exhaled in an attempt to calm down. At least I was about to eat. As I relaxed at my usual table, surrounded by my cabinmates, I became aware of an argument. Thorin Oakenshield was yelling, "Saruman is not a more powerful wizard than Voldemort . . ."

Hearing that, I almost returned to my gloomy thoughts, but Josh cut in. "You have warts?"

"No, Josh," Thorin explained. "I said Volde*mort*, not *wart*."

"I have warts, too," Josh continued. "I have a big one in my armpit. Take a look . . ."

"Do you want to see *my* armpit?" Stinky asked.

"NO!" we all answered at once.

Thankfully, he didn't gas us out. Instead he said, "Here comes Gertrude with the menu board!"

Gertrude turned the board so the mess hall could read tonight's dinner. Stinky gasped, "My favorites. Clam chowder followed by spaghetti with clam sauce."

So *that* was Mr. Periwinkle's money-saving scheme. I pictured the dirty zebra mussels and could feel myself gagging as I stormed out the door.

My horrid day fueled my pen that evening. Sitting in the cabin after dinner, I wrote a letter to my parents listing seventeen reasons why they needed to drop everything and get me out of Camp Wy-Mee. Then I started another letter. This one was to the girl I hoped was still my girlfriend.

Dear Jessica,

I've tried to find ways to call, text, or email you, but I think my parents accidentally sent me to jail instead of camp. The good news is that I'll be home real soon. I imagine my parents will be picking me up just a few hours after you read this. I can't wait to do all the things we talked about doing. I miss you.

Rodney

I sealed the envelope and tucked both letters under my pillow. Lying back in bed with my hands cradling my head, I smiled while listening to the sounds of a camp summer night. Crickets and bugs chirped and buzzed. Woo hummed jazz softly from his chair. Thorin practiced spells on Harry the Raccoon. Josh laughed at him. Fernando's comb swished back and forth through his hair as he winked at himself in the mirror. It was all music to my ears, as I knew that real soon, I'd be out of here.

The following day I dropped the letters in the mailbox outside the door of the dining hall. I whispered a little adios to Camp Wy-Mee and walked down toward the fields. It was a sunny, cool morning. The whole world seemed divided into blue and green—the big blue sky over the blue lake, surrounded by green trees and greener grass. Before moving to Garrettsville, I had grown up near New York City, and we never had mornings like this. Something hit me, and for a second I saw the world through Mr. Periwinkle's eyes. With the sun on my face and the smell of clover in the air, I felt momentarily sad about leaving.

"Amigo, get over here!"

It was Fernando calling out to me. He sat above the fields on a grassy spot between two girls. I smiled and walked up to them.

"Rodney, I want you to meet Alison and Megan. Alison and Megan, this is Rodney Rathbone." They both smiled. Megan's attention immediately went back to Fernando's hair, but Alison held my gaze for a second.

"Nice to meet you both," I said, "but I'm leaving camp."

Fernando looked surprised. "Why the rush to leave, Rodney? As you can see, there are certain advantages to camp life." His eyes darted sideways at the girls. He had a point there. He stood up and grabbed my shoulder. "Girls, pardon me for one moment. Rodney, walk with me. We must talk."

We strolled slowly along the path toward the beech tree where Periwinkle had found me the day before. "What would I do without you?" Fernando asked. "Sure, there are lots of pretty girls here, but I need a buddy to share in the excitement. Now, I admit that Josh is, shall we say, entertaining, but the conversations are limited. As for Stinky, well, normally I'd be impressed with a guy that makes girls faint, but I don't think suffocating body odor is the way to a girl's heart. Then there's Thorin. He's smarter than any of us, I suspect, but I don't speak Klingon or Na'vi, so I'm lost half the time. All I got is you, my man."

I hadn't thought about it that way. I had made a good friend, and I'd be missed when I left. "Yeah, well, I already sent the letters." I felt a little bad. "Besides, a lot of people have it in for me. Do you think it's legal to send someone under a boat to scrape off the camp's dinner? Thorin Oakenshield told me zebra mussels are full of pollutants. The Periwinkles are torturing me *and* poisoning the camp."

"I wouldn't worry. Things are looking up." Fernando's eyes were fixed over my shoulder. I turned and my heart began to beat a little faster. In a hushed voice, he observed, "Excitement seems to follow you, Rodney. I want to join you on the ride."

My attention was now on Tabitha, who had come right up to us. She stood before me, looking down at her sandal as it slowly traced an imaginary line in the grass. "Hi, Rodney. I hear we're in athletics class together."

"Uh, yeah, um, that's what Mr. Periwinkle said." My mind went blank. Fernando cleared his throat and motioned in the direction of the athletics fields. My wits returned. "We have class now, right? Maybe we could walk together?"

Before she could answer, Fernando chimed in, "Ah

yes, a summer stroll across the fields. Can't you just smell it? The air is intoxicating. Time for Fernando to be heading off."

He ducked away, leaving me nervous. I could feel my cheeks getting hot.

Tabitha had an eyebrow raised in Fernando's direction. "What's with your friend?"

Before I could answer or make some joke, she shifted her gaze back to me. Her look was intense, yet playful. Her green eyes swept me into another world.

"You know, Rodney, you and I haven't been alone together since signing up for sailing class." She took a step closer. I was about to float away or throw up, I wasn't sure which. I tried to gain control of myself. "What's the matter?" she asked. "Don't you like me?"

"Like you?" My voice cracked. "Sure I like you."

"Hey, Tabitha! Oh, I see you're busy studying the lower classes again." It was Todd, darn it! He rode up to us on some weird contraption that looked like a motorized pogo stick on wheels. "Like my Segway x2 Personal Transporter? Just had it dropped off."

"From where, Mars?" I asked.

"You know, there's something interesting about him, isn't there, Tabitha?" He talked as if I wasn't even there, or like I was some animal who couldn't understand him. "Anyway, want to ride on my Segway to athletics? It's all the way across those long fields."

I was about to tell him not to waste his time, that

Tabitha and I shared a special connection . . .

"Okay, Todd. *Awesome.*"

A knife sliced into my heart. Hurt and disgusted, I watched as she went up to him, looking slightly unsure of how to climb on.

"Just step up on the platform," Todd began. Then he smiled at me and said, "Tabitha, put your arms around me and hold on tight. That's it." With a little hidden wink in my direction, he added, "Tighter, Tabitha. I don't want you to fall off."

His smile made me sick and full of bitterness. I watched them zoom off across the fields. Yes, I knew I was soon leaving camp, and I hoped Jessica was waiting for me at home, but seeing Tabitha ride off with Big Jerk Number One made my stomach ache. I turned and walked back toward Fernando. "What were you saying about things looking up?"

He had pretty much seen the whole thing and could only manage a feeble, "The day's not over, my friend."

"That's true," I agreed. "There's still plenty of time for me to scrub some rusty ship bottoms. Maybe Mrs. Periwinkle has a whole fleet waiting for me. Maybe a tree will land on me. Better yet, maybe at archery later I'll get shot in the butt by an arrow. I'm so relieved the day's not over. Lots to look forward to."

I stomped off to athletics, alone, holding on to the only good thing I had going for me. At least the letters were in the mail.

Chapter 10

MR. CRAMPS

"Hey, Rootbone!"

It was that idiot Magnus. Over the first week, I'd done a decent job at avoiding him, but now he was approaching as I neared the athletic field. I was tired and sweaty from the long walk and in no mood to deal with him. I put my head down and just kept going—until his massive hand thumped my chest so hard I almost fell backward.

"Not zo fast, Rootbone . . ."

"It's Rathbone," I gasped.

"Dat's nice. Anyvay, thought you'd vant to know I have taken every class vis Mr. Cramps for twelve years. You could say I'm vis him always very much." Maybe his sentences came out so weird from all the raw eggs he put in his smoothies. He continued, "I told him about you and you know vat Mr. Cramps said?"

"That he's sick of you being vis him always very much?"

He rolled his neck, which crunched several times. "He told me he'd take special interest in you. Now, you go!" He gave me a hard pat on the back, laughed, and marched off.

As I approached the class I noticed a bunch of kids sitting in front of a nasty-looking older guy, who I guessed was the famous Mr. Cramps. Todd was lying on his side, poking Tabitha in the leg. She was swatting his hand, but smiling. I bit my lip in anger.

"You're late!" The crazy old guy was yelling at me. This was the last thing I needed right now. I turned around and stared at him. Like two gunfighters from a western, we took a moment to size each other up. He looked older—in his fifties or sixties—but he looked like he'd spent the last half century doing push-ups and arm wrestling. His gray hair was pulled back and his eyes burned fiercely into mine. Suddenly a breeze hit and his hair floated up from behind his head, revealing a big bald spot. I watched the hair momentarily wave in the breeze before he slapped it back down. I half expected him to start yelling at the wind. I mean, this guy looked nuts. His tight polyester gym-teacher shorts and high white socks didn't help.

And I knew right then, right before I noticed the muscle in his cheek twitch and his lips begin to part, before he uttered another word—I knew I was facing an enemy. Another enemy in a long year crammed with enemies. His words confirmed my belief. "I said, you're late! Now give me twenty!"

"I didn't bring any money with me," I replied.

Mr. Cramps smacked his forehead and pushed his fingers up through his hair. "Boy, are you thick or something?" he asked, quickly plastering his hair back down to cover his scalp. "Now do twenty push-ups!" I didn't argue. As I went up and down, Mr. Cramps counted and commented, "Don't raise your rear in the air!"

"I don't think he's going down far enough," Todd added.

"You're right, Vanderdick. All the way down, new kid!" Todd choked from laughter. Finally, Mr. Cramps called, "Twenty!" and I collapsed.

"Now, that pathetic little demonstration proves my point," Cramps instructed the crowd. "Kids today are weak and undisciplined. Fortunately for you runts, you have taken this class. Your days of video game playing, chicken nugget eating, book reading, and whining to your mommies are over! I *guarantee* . . . I will personally make men out of all of you!"

"But some of us are girls."

"That won't stop me!" Several of the girls looked at each other. "Now then, any more dopey questions?"

"Just one," I volunteered. "Did you forget to take your medication this morning?" It was out of my mouth before I knew what I was saying. My big dumb mouth. Mr. Cramps's gray eyes bored into mine and he got close to my face. I could see a vein begin to throb in his neck.

"You're that Bone kid, right?"

"Rathbone."

"Well, I sure am going to enjoy this. Yessiree. Every one of you, line up! We're going for a little jog."

Lounging on the ground, Todd called out, "Excuse me, Mr. Cramps. I sprained my ankle getting off my Segway, so I think I'll need to sit this one out." He rubbed his ankle twice and winked at Tabitha. Mr. Cramps's face tightened, and he opened his mouth, but Todd beat him to it. "You're enjoying the new baseball backstop and soccer goals my dad donated, right? I called my dad and told him to talk to Mr. Periwinkle about resurfacing the basketball court."

Mr. Cramps chewed on his plastic whistle.

Todd added, "I'm sure he'll do it, after I tell him what a wonderful instructor you are. By the way, Tabitha here is helping me keep my foot elevated." Todd placed his foot into Tabitha's lap. "It's all right if she sits out, too, right?"

Crack!! Mr. Cramps bit right through his whistle. Suddenly his hair began to blow wildly in the wind. He took a couple of deep breaths, spit a few pieces of broken whistle in the air, and grumbled, "Okay."

I thought it was worth a shot. "You know, Mr. Cramps, my *knee* seems . . ."

"MOVE IT, RAT TRAP!!!"

I took off running. The rest of the class, minus Todd and Tabitha, did too.

75

★ ★ ★

Now most gym teachers I've been around stand and give orders and watch us from afar. Well, Mr. Cramps wasn't like them. Every twenty or so yards he'd run up and shout something in my direction. "Quicker, Rathbone! My grandmother moves faster than you… and she's dead!" He was crazy, and out to get me. I figured Magnus had played a part in it all.

We were running laps around the perimeter of the large fields. Sweat dripped into my eyes and my lungs burned. The third time around the fields, Mr. Cramps decided to start running right in back of me. I could barely breathe. I eyed Todd and Tabitha as we ran past. Todd yelled out, "Looking good, Rathbone!"

"Don't listen to your friend. You look *pathetic*!" Cramps barked in my ear.

I continued running, thinking the whole time I should just run straight into the woods and keep going till I found the highway home. I couldn't take it anymore. Somehow I was moving, but my legs felt like they were about to give out.

"Don't slow down, boy!" Cramps shouted from behind. He was now two feet behind me and with every step seemed to be gaining ground. We were coming up to Todd and Tabitha again. I could see them talking and laughing, and this time I strained to hear what he was saying. I wish I hadn't.

"Tabitha, I made you this clover necklace. The

next one I give you will be made of diamonds."

It was the last straw. I stopped dead in my tracks. I don't know if I was about to ask Tabitha how she could be with such a loser, or if my legs just gave out, but I stopped short and kind of fell to the ground. And that's when it happened. Mr. Cramps ran right into my head. Immediately the air was filled with shouts of pain as he cupped his belly—well, several inches below his belly. He looked at me. His face was red as a tomato, his eyes bulged, and he stammered, "You! You, you . . ."

He stopped. Mr. Periwinkle had popped out from behind a bush.

"Oh, splendid! You two are becoming fast friends. Rodney, did you know that Mr. Cramps here has won two Ironman Triathlons? Who better to train with? What do you think, Eugene? A future marathoner here in young Rodney?"

Mr. Cramps managed a grin. "Well, Percy," he answered, "he'll either become a great runner, or he'll *die* trying."

I hoped Periwinkle could see he was crazy and save me, but he said, "Do you hear that, Rodney? Your camp experience just keeps getting better. To think, a little while ago you wanted to leave us."

He stood there beaming for a moment, then seemed to regain his purpose. "Oh yes. I know you're biting at the chomp to get back to running, but I came down here to talk to you both. Maybe Todd could join us, too.

Todd, come over here, please." We watched Todd limp exaggeratedly over to us. "Nothing serious, I hope?" Periwinkle asked him.

"Nothing a little rest won't cure."

"Oh, thank heavens. Anyway, Mrs. Periwinkle has come up with a splendid idea. Eugene, she wants you to run a softball game between the Algonquin and Cherokee cabins. Todd, Rodney, you can be captains. Won't that be fun?" Before we had a chance to answer he continued, "I'm glad you all like the idea. We'll play the game Friday after dinner. The rest of the camp can watch. Mrs. Periwinkle will be sure to be there. Maybe the excitement will get her to change her mind about . . ." He looked at us nervously for a second, then, noticing Todd's ride gleaming in the sun, changed the subject. "Todd, what is that thing you have over there?"

"Mr. Periwinkle, *that* is my new Segway Transporter."

"Ahh, well, campers aren't allowed to have motorized vehicles in camp, and . . ."

Todd looked pained. "Oh, that's a shame, Mr. Periwinkle. I asked my dad to send you one, too, courtesy of Vanderdick Enterprises."

"Oh really?" A bright smile burst onto Periwinkle's face. "Why don't you show me how it works?"

The two of them walked off, leaving me alone with Cramps. I felt like I better say something. "Uh, sorry about hitting you in the, you know . . ."

He didn't answer. He seemed to be deep in thought. Then he smiled an evil grin. "A little softball game Friday night, huh? I have to hand it to Mrs. Periwinkle. Yes, something tells me it will be a real fun time."

A gleam in his eye told me it would be anything but.

Chapter 11

MIDNIGHT MADNESS

I clapped my hands twice. "More grapes." Tabitha walked over to me, bringing the green fruit. I plucked one. Then I turned to look at Jessica. She was fanning me with a large palm leaf. The breeze blew gently through my hair and I leaned back on my throne, feeling completely relaxed and happy. Someone tapped me on the head. I sighed. "Girls, girls, no more grapes right now. The prince needs his beauty rest . . ."

"Uh, it's time to go, Rodney. Everyone's asleep."

"Huh?" My eyes opened into darkness. I became aware that Fernando was leaning over me.

"You're dreaming about grapes?" he asked.

No! It was only a dream. I wanted to roll over and cry into my pillow. Maybe if I fell back to sleep, the dream would come back.

"Come on, let's go."

"You go. I was having the best dream . . ."

"Shhh, you'll wake Woo."

Every part of me wanted to stay in the bunk bed. My sleeping bag felt warm against the evening chill and I slid lower into it, hoping Fernando would go away. I had promised to go with him on a midnight mission to sneak into the girls' division. I was supposed to have stayed awake until everyone else dropped off to sleep, but I had dozed off, too.

Fernando shook my shoulder. "Come on, Rodney. Alison actually said I wasn't man enough to visit her in the night. Fernando not man enough! Can you imagine?"

"Well, you *are* only twelve," I responded groggily.

"Just the idea makes my skin crawl. Wild horses couldn't stop me now, but I need backup. And besides, I'm not going to let you mope around here for the next few days thinking about Tabitha. *Vaminos!*"

Tabitha. Hearing her name sent two emotions racing through me. One was anger. I was mad at the way she had acted on the soccer field. The other emotion, though, was anything but anger. She sure looked good walking with the grapes, and even though she was in a different cabin than Alison, maybe we'd see her tonight. I sat up and pulled my legs over the side of the bed. I was already dressed in my darkest clothes. I put on my sneakers and started to walk with Fernando out the cabin door.

"Where ya goin'?"

Fernando and I jumped. Josh was looking down at us from his bunk. "To the bathroom," I whispered. "Go back to sleep."

We were fully clothed in black outfits. Fernando had a bandana tied around his head. Josh's face scrunched up and his brain seemed to be struggling with something. "Uhhhhh . . ."

"Not so loud," I whispered.

"Uhhhh . . ."

Fernando spoke up. "Josh, if you must know, we're sneaking into the girls' division."

"I like girls," he announced.

Fernando's eyes flashed in the dark. "Rodney, you hear his enthusiasm? You could learn a thing or two from this one." I looked over at Josh. Apart from punching walls and setting bugs on fire, I wondered what enlightening things he could share with me. "Would you like to come with us?" Fernando asked him.

"Pretty ones going to be there?"

"I love this guy. We must be brothers. Climb down here and let's go."

And with that, the three of us headed off into the night.

Winding our way between the dark cabins, I whispered, "There's the Algonquin cabin. We can't make any noise."

While Fernando and I made our way past the cabins like two ninjas, Josh stomped like a rhino, cracked sticks, and kicked up crinkly, dry leaves. Fernando gave me a strained look.

"Hey, he's *your* brother," I reminded him.

He opened his mouth to reply, but it was Magnus who spoke next. "Iss zomebody out there?" he shouted.

For a second we froze in our tracks. Then, in a high, scratchy voice, I answered, "Just Gertrude and Alice!" A light went on in the cabin and we heard the screen door swing open. The three of us burst out laughing and broke into a run toward the woods.

"Goot back here!" Magnus demanded, but it was too late. We were now tearing along Scalped Indian Path.

"Hey, Rodney, you do a pretty good girl's voice," Fernando teased.

"You think?" I laughed. We slowed down a bit as we entered the woods. We had chosen this path earlier in the day while plotting the adventure, but at night it was a bit creepy. The trail ended at the soccer field, and from there it was just a stroll across the grass to the girls' cabins.

We moved on through the dark woods without talking. In the past, this would have been the point where my legs started shaking, but I knew the scariest thing in the woods tonight was the big goon grunting behind me. Actually, I was happy to have Josh along. The thought made me smile. Just a few weeks ago he'd have been the last guy on the planet I would have chosen to be alone with in the pitch-black woods.

Fernando interrupted my thoughts. "Listen, it's nights like this that you'll remember for the rest of your life." I smiled. Sometimes he sounded like he was twelve going on sixty. "Take a moment to soak it in. Smell the night air . . ."

I inhaled deeply through my nose. There was a strong scent of pine needles, and then a stronger scent of—"Awwwwww! Gross!"

"Like that, Rodney?" Josh grinned. "Just like my favorite song. *Beans, beans, good for the ear, the more you eat them, the more you stink. The more you stink, the more you drink, the more you drink, the more you pee, so eat all them beans!*"

"Interesting version," I commented, holding my nose. Seeing the trees thinning up ahead, I added, "There's the field."

We walked up to the edge of the forest. The soccer field looked different in the dark. One nice difference was that Mr. Cramps wasn't there yelling at us with his crazy hair flying around, but the change went beyond that. Everything was really still. The goalposts stood out in the darkness and the white lines on the grass looked like they were floating in space. On the other side of the field, a big orange moon hung just above the tops of the trees. It was a beautiful summer night and now that a fresh breeze was blowing—and Josh was safely behind me on the trail—I took a chance and breathed it all in.

As if reading my mind, Fernando said, "This place is pretty cool." Then, remembering why we were there, he added, "Just think, boys, our destiny awaits us on the other side of that field."

We walked on silently and were halfway across when a massive beam from a flashlight blazed in our direction. "Down!" I hissed.

We dropped and lay flat. I could see the beam moving across the grass. It slid over our heads. *Magnus*, I thought. I should have known the big, evil jerk would come after us. What was his problem? The light made it to the end of the field and doubled back. Lying still, we waited. The beam lit up our patch of ground, and I prayed our black clothes would blend in with the grass. I watched it reach the other side of the rectangular field and click off. After a couple of tense minutes we moved forward, crouching on the balls of our feet, ready to drop at a moment's notice.

And that's when it hit me—the real reason why I didn't want to get caught. I was afraid they would kick me out of camp! Had I suddenly gone crazy? For days, all I wanted to do was leave here, but this midnight mission had somehow changed all that. Despite Todd and Magnus, I was beginning to enjoy Camp Wy-Mee. In fact, I was having the time of my life.

As we continued on, however, a feeling of regret began to worm its way to the back of my head. If only I hadn't sent that letter to my parents . . .

Chapter 12

THE GIRL NO ONE EXPECTED

When we reached the girls' division, the cabins were eerily silent. The only sign of life was in the distance—some moths circling a lightbulb outside the girls' bathroom. But by us it was dark and every cabin looked the same. "Which one?" I whispered.

"Don't worry, when it comes to the ladies, Fernando always finds his way." He held his finger up in the breeze. "That one. Let's go."

We snuck our way from cabin shadow to rock to bush to tree and eventually arrived at the door of Alison's cabin. Fernando winked. "The journey will all have been worth it in a second." He slowly pulled the screen door open and we stepped into the lavender-scented dark. I heard the breathing of a dozen sleeping girls. As my brain digested the enormity of entering such an unfamiliar, magical place, I got a little dizzy and almost toppled to the floor. Fernando grabbed my arm. "Steady, big fella," he whispered.

A voice floated to us from a top bunk on the left. "I never thought you would actually show." Even in the dark, I could see Alison's red hair hanging down.

Fernando's white smile gleamed with satisfaction. "It is always a mistake to underestimate Fernando."

Alison whispered, "I should have known better," and quietly swung down from her bunk. "Girls, wake up. We have visitors." Shapes shifted in the dark. My pulse quickened as girls stirred and climbed from their beds. Several flashlights clicked on and one went right into my eyes and stayed there. I felt like a prisoner about to be interrogated.

"He's cute." Some girl giggled. I could live with this kind of interrogation.

"And check out the muscles on that one," another girl added. "Look at these three — our knights in shining armor."

Fernando raised a pleased eyebrow in my direction. One girl went up to Josh. "What's your name?"

"Josh."

"You look very strong."

"You want me to break something?"

"Charming, too," she said in a giggle to her friend.

Fernando pulled out a bottle of Coke he had been hiding. "Ladies, I've been saving this bottle of bubbly for an occasion like this." He turned the cap. The soda instantly foamed up and blasted out in all directions.

"How romantic." Alison smirked, wiping the drink

from her forehead. Then, to me she added, "Rodney, I'm surprised you're not poking around in Tabitha's cabin."

Now, that thought had certainly occurred to me, but I'd been around Fernando long enough to know how to play it. "Who?" I asked.

Alison rolled her eyes.

Wrrreeeeee! Suddenly the screen door creaked open. I could see Mrs. Periwinkle and a counselor or two about to enter. Fernando gave a quick bow. "Ladies, another time." He climbed across Alison's bed, lifted the window screen, and slid out into the night. Josh scrambled after him, showing some rare alertness.

I was too far from the opening and realized I wouldn't make it. I weaseled my way into a small alcove between two bunk beds just as Mrs. Periwinkle entered the room.

From my hiding spot, I could see her standing with a large flashlight. A strangely familiar sense of dread crept down my spine. "What is going on in here?" she demanded. The girls, who had jumped back into bed, pretended to wake up. It would be a miracle if she didn't spot me. I squirmed into the smallest space I could find. "I *repeat*, what is going on in here?"

Alison spoke up. "Mrs. Periwinkle, what do you mean? We were asleep."

I held my breath and watched. Mrs. Periwinkle's curly hair cast an eerie glow as she blasted the beam at Alison. "Young lady, I had a report that some boys were on the prowl. I'm checking all the cabins." She paused, then added, "I guess I was mistaken. Hold on. What is that all over the floor?" It was the Coke. She squatted down, looking just like a detective at a crime scene. She touched the soda and applied a drop to the end of her tongue. Her eyes hardened and she spat. "I taste misbehaving!" Then she slowly began moving her flashlight along the walls of the room. I knew it was only a matter of seconds before it reached my hiding spot.

"Here," Alison whispered, tossing me what looked like a dead rat. "It's a wig from last year's show."

Mrs. Periwinkle's light was almost upon me now. I stuck the thing on my head and threw a blanket over my shoulders.

"Who is that?" The flashlight was now pointed right at me. I was caught! I was doomed. "Who are you?" Mrs. Periwinkle demanded. "What are you doing over there?"

No one spoke. You could hear a pine needle drop. "Me?" I finally answered, putting on a high-pitched girl's voice. "I'm Alison's cousin." I had suddenly remembered Fernando teasing me about imitating Gertrude and Alice. I figured I had nothing to lose. "You remember me, Mrs. Periwinkle, don't you?"

She looked confused and annoyed. "What's your name again?"

"Rod . . . Rodweena."

"Rodweena what?"

"Raa . . . uhhh . . . Smith."

"Rodweena Raauhhhsmith." She seemed to ponder this. "Interesting name." Her eyes were squinting and I knew the charade was almost up. I prayed the rat-wig thing didn't fall off my head.

"Yes," I continued. "A most peculiar name. From my mother's side. Anyway, thank you for trying to capture the boys. I can't imagine anything worse than some smelly boys snooping about."

Mrs. Periwinkle seemed to soften. "Yes, I agree. And these *particular* boys I'm after are most undesirable."

"Oh, I'm sure they must be," I continued. "Anyone who would turn down a good night's rest to violate camp rules must be on a sure path to delinquency." I was on a roll now. "I sincerely hope you capture them and punish them *severely*." Maybe I had gone too far. Mrs. Periwinkle was looking at me intently and I gulped quietly.

"Well, Rodweena," she announced, "It is an absolute pleasure meeting you again. It's gratifying to see a proper young lady with a good head on her shoulders. And so pretty! I wish more of these girls had your sensibilities. Good night."

Just then the door screeched open. "Mrs. Periwinkle, we found these two snooping about." A counselor brought in Fernando and Josh.

The Periwinkle sneer was back. "So, you thought you could sneak into the girls' division? Well, as you can see, breaking the rules is not a wise thing to do. You're looking at a significant punishment. What do you have to say for yourselves?"

Before they could answer, I asked in my high voice, "Are these the two ruffians?"

Fernando and Josh noticed me for the first time and I thought Fernando's eyes were going to pop out of his head. He bit his lip to keep from laughing, but in an instant recovered his usual nonchalant cool. Josh, on the other hand, studied me closely, slowly tilting his head from side to side like a confused dog. I gulped. He was about to blow my cover. He opened his mouth and I cringed.

"Stop staring at Rodweena, you!" Mrs. Periwinkle scolded. "You're in enough hot water without upsetting this poor girl!"

Fernando strode forward and grabbed Mrs. Periwinkle's hand. "Pardon me, madame." She tried to shake off his grip, but he held tight and said, "I'm very sorry to break any rules, but ever since the first time I saw you atop your beautiful horse, I haven't been able to get you out of my mind." Now it was my turn to keep from laughing as Fernando inched closer to her. I noticed Mrs. Periwinkle had stopped shaking her arm. "Hagatha—may I call you that? Such a beautiful name deserves to be said aloud."

I expected Mrs. Periwinkle to slap him, but she was still looking almost mesmerized. Fernando went on. "I looked out at the beautiful moon and night sky tonight. It made me think of you, and it was all too much for me." He took her hand and placed her palm against his chest. "It drove me mad. Mad, I say! I knew I had to see you." It was hard to tell in the dark, but Mrs. Periwinkle looked flushed. "Punish me if you must," Fernando went on. "It was worth it. Being here with you now is worth any sacrifice."

Mrs. Periwinkle swayed on her feet and one of the counselors steadied her. Shakily she said, "Yes, well . . ."

"Fernando."

"Of course. Fernando, why don't we speak tomorrow and we'll discuss the . . . errrr . . . punishment." Something told me he wasn't going to be scraping zebra mussels off her boat.

Fernando hadn't finished. "Oh, and just so you know, the only reason Josh was out tonight was because he was trying to stop me. But stopping this feeling is like trying to stop a locomotive."

At this point the attention returned to Josh. His gaze was still fixed on me and his dopey look seemed more focused than usual. I cringed. He was going to give me away for sure. What he said next, however, was just as bad.

"Uhh . . . hi. I'm Josh." He took a step in my direction. I saw that he was blushing. "You sure are pretty. Could we, uh, get married or something?"

Chapter 13

STRIKES AND BALLS

"Hey, lay it on down, toe lappers. You got the chaws. Dig?"

No, we didn't dig. We were pretty far from digging. But Woo was our team's softball manager, so we nodded like we knew what he was talking about.

"Don't let no haze hang the cabeza. Go out there and lay it on nice and thick. You dig, Rodney?"

"Uhh . . . you're saying . . . play hard?"

"Hey now, make the bugs dance, young men with bats!" He waved for us to go out onto the field.

So, armed with the strangest pep talk in history, we ran to our positions. Josh was on first, Thorin on second, Fernando on third, Stinky ran out to play catcher, but Gabe, the head of the boys division and today's umpire, began gagging and switched Stinky to centerfield. Mr. Cramps pitched and I took my spot at shortstop. The rest of the cabin filled the outfield. Someone who made me very nervous, however, had appointed himself pitcher—for both teams.

As if sensing my unease, Mr. Cramps turned toward me and called out, "I've been looking forward to this game." He was smiling but didn't look at all happy. I could feel the wickedness pouring out of him, and my stomach twisted as I pondered what he meant.

A counselor named Gabe yelled, "Play ball!" Mr. Periwinkle stood on a hill near first base, surrounded by the whole camp. He looked like a kid on opening day. Unable to contain his excitement, he reached out and grasped his wife's shoulder. His hand was abruptly swatted as if it was a mosquito. Mrs. Periwinkle looked completely annoyed, kind of like she was inhaling the air next to Stinky. Her expression changed and her cheeks darkened, however, when Fernando passed by, smiling in her direction.

I kicked the dirt and tried to focus my thoughts. I'd had a lot of fun the other night. After the counselors took Josh and Fernando away, I said good-bye to Alison and the girls and made my way back to the cabin. When I finally got there, Josh couldn't stop talking about Rodweena. Fernando kept egging him on.

"Tell Rodney how pretty she was!" I wanted to punch him, but the whole thing was so funny that I just went along with it. In fact, Fernando had been right when he said I would never forget the evening. It cemented the belief that I liked camp and wanted to stay. And now, knowing that I wanted to be here, my main goal was to win this game and beat Todd and Magnus.

I looked at the two hundred or so kids and counselors sitting around the camp's first couple. My stomach felt uneasy and my palms began to sweat. If four hundred eyes staring at us weren't enough, I couldn't help but notice one particularly devilish pair looking my way. They were accompanied by a slight, sly grin on full lips and dark brown hair. I tried to shake it off, figuring she was probably giving similar looks to Todd.

I pounded my fist into my mitt and looked up for the first time to inspect our opponents. I gulped. *Who had invited the New York Yankees?* All right, they weren't quite the Yankees, but seeing the Algonquins stretching, taking some practice swings, and wearing gleaming pinstriped uniforms, they sure looked the part. As Magnus brought them together for a pregame conference, I realized we weren't in their league—not by a long shot. Without exception, they were big and athletic. Any swagger I possessed evaporated like a puddle in the Sahara. As the first inning got underway, I wasn't surprised to see things go quickly downhill.

Mr. Cramps began the game with a slow, soft floater to an Algonquin named Biff. Biff's bat smacked a hard grounder right at Thorin Oakenshield. My jaw dropped as he caught it. Thorin pivoted and threw the ball to first. Josh stood looking blank and made no move to catch it. The ball bounced off the side of his skull with a hollow thud. Biff was safe. Josh's expression changed from dumb to dumb and *angry*. He started to charge Thorin. I blocked his way before our dwarf-wizard second baseman was pounded into the dirt.

"Josh, you got to catch the ball, then get the runner out," I said quickly. "Catch. You get it?"

He looked from Thorin to me. "Catch ball and get runner."

"Yes. See that kid with the bat? That's who you get."

Josh nodded vaguely and walked back to first base.

I turned to Thorin. "Nice play."

"I'll have you know, I'm an all-star seeker for my Quidditch team."

Well, that's comforting news, I thought to myself.

Another Algonquin, Chip, was waiting in the batter's box. He was laughing with Todd and the other guys about Josh's play. They settled down and Mr. Cramps again threw an excruciatingly slow toss that a kindergartner could have laced. Chip made contact and sent the ball bouncing toward my side of the infield. I felt the adrenaline pump through my veins as I dashed to the left. Reaching down, I was relieved to feel the ball collide with the inside of my mitt. I shifted my feet and made a perfect throw to first, all the while hoping that Tabitha was paying attention. Josh was ready this time and caught the ball. Then he yelled, "Get runner!" Next thing I knew he ran right at Chip, yanked him off the ground and body-slammed him into foul territory.

The result was pandemonium. Magnus went berserk, and after some discussion the runner was declared out, which made Magnus even crazier. He looked like an insane Viking as he screamed at Gabe and tried to grab Josh. It was nice to see him so upset, but I have to admit he had a point. In the end, he calmed down after Gabe moved Josh out to left field. Play continued.

Todd walked to the plate. He smiled and waved to the crowd. Most of them ignored him, but Mrs. Periwinkle clapped slightly. *Funny how evil sticks together,* I thought.

Mr. Cramps flipped Todd a nice, easy pitch. He didn't swing. "A little lower, if you don't mind?"

Mr. Cramps nodded and tossed a ball that was slow and sweet and right in Todd's wheelhouse. He drilled it. I watched it fly out over the infield, right to center field. Right at Stinky. I held my breath.

Stinky looked up. Seeing the ball flying his way, he covered his head and flung himself to the ground as if the softball was a grenade. The ball missed him and rolled way out toward the woods. Todd was rounding third before anyone even picked it up. I stood there watching Tabitha and the Algonquins cheer their captain as he stepped on home, making it a two-nothing game.

Somehow we started to play some defense and got the next two outs, but things didn't improve when it was our turn to bat. Thorin Oakenshield led off. I watched him pull out a wand and head to the batter's box.

"You can't use that. It's too light," I said, stopping him. "Get a bat."

"I'll have you know, Rodney, this wand is eleven inches. It's made from holly and has a phoenix feather inside. Nice and supple!" He swished it over my head. My hair tingled as it flew past. That was the end of the conversation, and he stepped into the box amid laughs and taunts from the Algonquins.

I turned to Fernando. "I thought you said he was smart."

"I figured he was because he reads a lot." He shrugged. "Evidently there's a difference."

Mr. Cramps wound up his arm and threw a very quick, hard toss towards the plate. I cursed to myself as I realized it was nothing like the lazy lollipops he'd tossed the Algonquins. Thorin Oakenshield swung his wand—which shattered the second it made contact with the ball.

"Haa haaa veery goooot!" Magnus's laugh boomed. Almost everyone else was laughing, too.

Thorin looked down at the splinters then turned back to me. "I don't understand. They say the wand picks the wizard. It spoke to me."

"What did it say? Stay away from baseball?" I led him aside. "Listen, why don't you have a conversation with one of these nice baseball bats?"

He stood there looking blank and dejected. I could hear Todd calling us idiots from the field. I looked at him in his fancy pinstripes, being nasty for no real reason, and my blood sizzled. I really wanted to beat the big jerk. That would show Todd. I grabbed Thorin's shoulder. I knew I had to speak his language. "Look at this one. It's aluminum, probably has unicorn hair in it—no, I bet it has dragon scales . . ."

He grabbed me by the shirt. "Do you really think so?" Then his eyes narrowed. "How do you know?"

"Ah, well, look at the writing . . . it's from Louisville."

"So?"

"Surely you've heard about the recent dragon sightings in Louisville? It's all over the Internet." He didn't reply. He was looking at the bat, stroking it gently.

"I think it's speaking to me," he said, eyes beginning to glaze over.

"Sure it is. It's saying to go get a hit."

He got into the box and actually ripped a line drive. It would have been a nice hit, but Cramps, looking like an Olympic gymnast, flew high into the air and made an amazing grab. He somersaulted and sprang catlike to his feet. "You're out, elf boy!" Cramps' eyes blazed at us—at me in particular. It had already dawned on me that our pitcher wasn't going to give us a fair shake, but now, seeing that nasty grin of his, I knew he was out to make sure the Algonquins won.

The rest of the inning was more of the same: fast

pitches and great plays by Cramps. Stinky struck out on three pitches. I batted third. Twice Cramps aimed for my head and I had to dive to get out of the way. I glanced back at Fernando, who was lying near the bats along with his fans, Alison, Megan, and Danielle. "I think he's trying to kill me," I called over to him.

"Perhaps, but look at the bright side."

"What bright side?"

"I'm surrounded by beautiful women! Who could ask for anything more?"

My friend was no help and the Algonquins were having a ball. "Strike him out," Todd called from first base. I would have loved to silence them, but in the end I bounced a roller to second base. Biff tossed to Todd and I was out.

Things stayed pretty much the same for most of the game. We never scored and fell further behind. As we neared the bottom of the final inning, the score was four to nothing. We were lucky to be that close. Most of the crowd was talking and goofing around, having lost interest in the pathetic, lopsided affair. The Algonquins took the field laughing, while we, the losers, were living up to our nickname. Almost immediately, we made two outs, and I sat, dejected, waiting for the game to end.

Someone else on the field was having a better time. Seeing that Josh was up, Todd laughed from first base. "This should be good. What a perfect way to end this fiasco." While brilliant at pummeling wimps, Josh hadn't done much of anything yet in the batter's box—not counting the last time up when he threw his bat into center field, almost killing the second baseman.

Some in the crowd, ready for one final bit of comic relief, focused on the at-bat. Moments later, a shocked gasp rang out as Josh topped the ball and hit a grounder toward third. But instead of running, he just stood there.

"Run to first!" I yelled at him.

"Uhh . . . duhhhh . . ."

"Run that way!" I pointed. "Step on that white thing over there!"

Lumbering hard down the base path, he headed off toward Todd, who was waiting at the base for the throw from third. Todd's usual calm, arrogant expression changed to one of shaken fear as he saw Josh heading his way. I guess no one had actually explained to Josh that you're supposed to drop the bat. Todd was so rattled by the club-swinging caveman heading his way that he forgot about the incoming ball, which sailed out to left field. Josh stopped on first, looking proud of his accomplishment.

"Run to second!" I yelled. Before he could utter another "Duh" I added, "Over there. Step on that white thing." He took off again, and neither the shortstop nor the second baseman wanted anything to do with the bat-wielding madman. "Go to third!" I hollered. "Over there!" Josh kept running. "Now, run home!"

For a moment, Josh looked more puzzled than usual, but he kept running — right off the field and into the crowd. It looked like he was heading toward the camp exit. *Huh?* Then it hit me. "Not *your* home! Run to home plate. Step on this white thing!"

He wheeled back into the field and darted toward home. With red eyes, huge muscles that swung the bat around his head, and a frothing mouth, he was a fearsome sight. I wasn't surprised when the catcher, who had received the ball from second, uttered a piercing screech and took off to cower behind Magnus. Josh, triumphant, stepped on the plate.

"You did it, Josh! A home run! We're on the board." He looked down at the plate, confused. I didn't bother to explain. Fernando, Stinky, and Thorin were all patting him on the back and cheering. The crowd loved it.

Mr. Periwinkle called, "Good show!" Then I heard him utter to Mrs. Periwinkle, "I always knew there was something special about that one."

A lot of our team's excitement died when Todd reminded us that we were still down by three runs. Then he added, "And that ape can't bat for the rest of you."

But our excitement and, more importantly, our luck, didn't die completely. Fernando, much to the delight of his screeching personal cheerleaders and Mrs. Periwinkle, hit a grounder up the middle past a diving Mr. Cramps. Then Thorin Oakenshield, while screaming, "By the power of dragons!" laced a single to right field.

Next up, Stinky somehow managed to make contact with the ball. The result was an improbable blooper over Todd's head. He scrambled for the ball, but when the dust settled, the now-attentive crowd could see that Stinky was standing safe at first.

I cheered loudly and high-fived Woo. "We're not out of it!"

"No blues in that news," he replied.

If the next batter got a hit, we could possibly win this game. I imagined the look of horror on Todd's face if we pulled it off. I smiled, pleased with the vision. As I pondered the possibilities, I looked off into the branches of a high oak tree behind first base. It was a nice moment, but then my chicken sense tingled and I knew something was off. I glanced back around. The entire camp was staring at me. I looked down at myself. Was I having that dream again where I forget to put my pants on? Seeing my shorts where they should be, I was about to exhale in relief when certain realities smacked my brain. We were still losing by three. There were two outs and the bases were loaded. And most important . . . I was up.

Woo handed me a bat and said, "All right, big daddy, get a hit and you're the cat's meow, the dog's bow wow, and the karate man's ka-pow." I nodded dumbly as my knees started to shake.

Thorin Oakenshield must have noticed. He jogged over to me from second base and whispered, "Just close your eyes and let the Force be your guide."

Before anyone else could offer me weird advice, I started for the batter's box . . . very reluctantly. This wasn't the first reluctant walk of my life. I've had to approach haunted houses and the occasional biker den, and while this was only a summer softball game, it somehow felt just as awful.

Fortunately, someone was waiting at home plate to give me some words of encouragement. Mr. Cramps leaned down and his teeth flashed as he whispered, "Striking you out, with the whole camp watching, will be the highlight of my summer. I used to be the closer for the Toledo Mud Hens. That's triple-A ball. I can still hit over ninety miles an hour on the radar gun. Have fun." He smiled to the crowd and gave me a friendly, if rather hard, pat on the back. Many clapped for the display of sportsmanship.

Previously in the game, Mr. Cramps pitched underhand, which of course is the traditional way to toss a softball. Now, he stood like a big leaguer and threw at me overhand. I barely saw the ball.

"Strike one!" yelled Gabe.

Cramps winked at me as he caught the ball thrown back by the catcher. He wound up again. As the ball flew past, I swung. I felt nothing but air as the bat twirled around me.

"Strike two."

I debated what to do. Run away?

"Ready for the heat, Rathbone?" Mr. Cramps jeered.

I noticed him give a slight nod at Mrs. Periwinkle and couldn't help but feel they were in on this together. He took a few steps toward me from the mound and said in a low, sinister voice, "I sure am going to enjoy this."

He returned to the mound and I watched his leg kick up. His arm went into its windup. I knew there was no way I would be able to hit what was coming. Unless . . .

As the ball left his fingers, I remembered Thorin's advice. I shut my eyes, put everything into it, and swung for the fences. I could hear the bat slice through the air and was fully expecting it to keep going. Only something hard stopped it. I don't know whether it was the Force or dumb luck, but the bat had actually collided with the ball. I could both feel and hear that perfect crack. I opened my eyes. Instead of sailing out past the outfielder's head, as I had hoped, the ball shot like a laser right at the unsuspecting Mr. Cramps, hammering him in the belly. Um, actually several inches below the belly.

He let out a wail and crumpled to the ground. For a moment I stood in shock, then my mind caught on and I raced down the first-base line. Fernando, Thorin Oakenshield, and Stinky were rounding second and third and on their way home. I flew past second. Mr. Cramps was still rolling back and forth, screeching. Todd tried to grab the ball but was having a difficult time getting around the writhing gym teacher. I sailed past third and headed for home. Todd finally scooped up the ball and tossed it to the catcher—a second after my sneaker stomped down on home plate. We won, five to four.

I was met by the fellas and hoisted onto their shoulders. The camp was rocking. People were laughing and pointing.

I noticed Magnus beating his fists into the ground like a spoiled two-year-old. Todd was speeding away on his Segway. Mr. Periwinkle was hugging Mrs. Periwinkle, who was doing her best to pry him off. Tabitha was looking my way, smiling. I didn't know how to react to that. It was then that I noticed Mr. Cramps. He was still on the pitcher's mound, bent over and resting on one knee.

Having been carried around on shoulders before, I cut the celebration short and decided to have some real fun. I slid into the crowd and approached the insane athletics teacher. His face looked like a beet and his eyes were wet and angry. I bent over slightly and asked, "So?"

"So . . . what?" he growled through clenched teeth.

"So, did you enjoy the game?"

Chapter 14

NEWS FROM HOME

"Make way for Orcrist," shouted Thorin, "Orcrist the Goblin Cleaver!" He was leading the way home after the ball game, the aluminum bat held out in front of him as if it were a sword. "Orcrist shall be placed on my chest when I'm buried under the mountain."

"Sure." I laughed. "Whatever you want. You and Oatmeal earned—"

"Orcrist," he corrected me.

"Yeah, you and ol' Orcrist taught the Algonquins a lesson today. We all did!"

We were straggling along in back of Thorin, the most unlikely of victorious teams. It wasn't exactly a ticker-tape parade down Broadway, but it felt that way to us. The walk back to the cabin was filled with high fives and laughs. The camp was electric. Everyone was thrilled with the Algonquins' defeat.

It sure was nice, the so-called losers being

congratulated, but some of my cabinmates were having trouble with all the attention. Stinky, for instance, panicked as the crowd swarmed around him. He ran behind Woo, who told him, "Relax, Frankie boy. No worries for the son in the sun."

I shook my head slightly, thinking Stinky needed some help, but then I noticed someone who needed it a whole lot more. My eyes popped out as I saw Josh about to punch a fan.

"What are you doing?" I yelled. I ran over and grabbed Josh, saving some little blond kid from one heck of a blow.

"They whack me on the back, I whack them in the face!"

"No, Josh. A pat on the back is a way of saying, you know, 'Good job' or whatever."

"It is?" he asked.

I could see him thinking. His face scrunched up and his big forehead was creased with lines. Fernando noticed, too, and whispered to me, "Our friends may be a bit odd, but they never cease to make life interesting."

I thought about that later on in Loserville and smiled. Yes, my new friends sure knew how to keep things interesting. I climbed into bed and let my mind play over the events of the day. Most of it was pretty funny, but then I thought about Tabitha. I tossed and turned awhile. It's very confusing when you like someone you also dislike. I rolled over and missed Jessica more than ever. Now *there* was a girl who was pretty but also nice. Of course, Alison was nice, too . . .

Eventually the sounds of night and the breathing of my cabinmates soothed my restlessness. Before I closed my eyes, the last thing I saw was Thorin, aluminum bat lying proudly by his side.

Thanks to Fernando, Tabitha was still on my mind the following morning. Eating breakfast in the dining hall, he said, "That was a lot of fun yesterday. I think Tabitha liked the game, too."

"I have no idea if she did or didn't, and I don't care," I lied.

Fernando shifted his eyes, signaling for me to look left. There she was, across the room, staring at me with her big green eyes. The runny eggs turned in my stomach. I wanted to look away, but I couldn't. She was so pretty it hurt.

"Don't fight it, Rodney. The feisty ones are the most fun." Fernando was obviously enjoying himself. Then, more seriously, he said, "Admit it. You know you don't want to leave this place."

Still caught in the trance of her gaze, I nodded dumbly. Eventually my attention shifted back to Fernando, and for the first time I told him what I already knew myself. "You're right. I don't want to leave camp."

Before I had a chance to say any more, Gabe yelled, "Mail for Rathbone!" and dropped two envelopes onto my plate. "Let's see, I have another. This one's for . . . Fernando."

A fancy pink envelope seemed to float down to the table. Even from where I sat, I could smell the perfume coming off it.

"Your letter smells nice," Stinky said. For someone who stunk like a dead fish, he sure seemed to appreciate a good scent.

"Chanel No. 5," Fernando replied, holding it to his nose.

I let the conversation fade and turned my attention to the two envelopes sitting in front of me. I eyed the first. With a sense of dread I saw it was from my parents. Would it say they were on their way to pick me up? Was this my last meal at Camp Wy-Mee? I lifted up the other letter. It was from . . . Jessica. My heart skipped a couple of beats. There's something about a handwritten letter. It's different than a text message, and I was excited to hold it. Did Jessica miss me? If she did, and I was being pulled out of here, leaving might not be so bad. All the questions and thoughts quickened my pulse and I felt short of breath. I exhaled and looked up at the ceiling. As my gaze made its way back down, Fernando asked, "Your parents?"

I nodded.

"And Jessica?"

I nodded again.

"Open them," he said.

I figured I'd read Jessica's letter when I was alone.

I stuck my finger into the corner of my parents' letter and ripped it open. I pulled out the folded stationery and noticed my mom's loopy handwriting. I gulped and began to read.

Dear Rodney,

We were so happy to receive your letter. We were even happier to read about how much you love Camp Wy-Mee.

Huh? I thought.

We are so pleased to hear that you've made so many friends, and that there are such nice counselors. It really seems like the people you mentioned, such as Mrs. Periwinkle and Magnus, have taken a special interest in you.

Was my mom losing it? I clearly said I hated them.

Knowing that there are kind, thoughtful people like them keeping an eye on you makes me very relieved. I was nervous about sending my baby away! It's also so nice that you've made a special friend in Todd.

Todd? What's going on? I never said that!

Anyway, your friend Toby has been asking about you. He said he and his older brother would be keeping an eye on you next fall in middle school. Isn't that thoughtful of him?

Aaaaarrgghhhhhh!

Well, I'd better go chase your father away from the little treat I've cooked up for you. We love you very much!

Love, Mom & Dad
P.S. I've been taking cooking classes, and the treat I mentioned was a batch of chocolate chip cookies that I hoped to bring up to you. But since you're having so much fun, we've decided to go on vacation with the Windbaggers to their house on lake Snore. We don't want to interrupt your fun. Oh, I would have mailed the cookies, but your dad ate them. Sorry, sweetie. Anyway, I'm sure camp food is delicious!

My jaw hung open as I reread and then reread again the words my mother had written. How in the world did she come up with that load of nonsense? My letter clearly described how much I hated camp, and especially hated Mrs. Periwinkle, Todd, and Magnus. I didn't fully believe my senses. I looked around the dining hall. Magnus was singing some bizarre song and pounding his fist on the table. Mr. Cramps was adjusting a bag of ice on his lap. Seeing me glance at him, he grabbed a piece of toast and took a savage bite. Mr. Periwinkle sat looking down on all of us with his usual beaming smile. Next to him sat Mrs. Periwinkle, who I noticed with alarm was glaring right at me. What was going on?

The bizarre, screwy letter from my mom messed with my brain. I had to read Jessica's letter right away. I ripped it open. As I unfolded the page, I caught a momentary whiff of her shampoo. It may not have been Chanel No. 5, but it sent a shiver down my spine. What I read almost sent my eggs back up my throat.

Dear Rodney,

I was very upset by your letter. I thought you really liked me. I can't believe you're breaking up with me! I almost cried when I read it but Toby reminded me that there are lots of other boys around. So you have fun at your camp and have a nice life.

Jess

It was the hammer blow. The page fell from my hand and my face landed with a thud on my plate.

"Wow, Rodney, you must be real hungry," Josh said. "Let me try eating like that." I heard what sounded like a pig eating from a trough, followed by, "Mmmmm."

Shakily, I lifted my head from the plate. Some egg fell from my cheek and landed in my lap. I was too upset to care.

"Let Fernando see," Fernando said. He picked up my letters and read both. When he was finished he set them down and looked at me.

"Well?" I asked.

"You're screwed."

"What?" I blurted.

"Someone is intercepting your mail. Devious move, too. Let's think about this. Do you have any enemies?"

The whole table cracked up laughing.

"Yes, silly question. Rodney here seems rather gifted at getting people to dislike him. Let's make a list."

"Mrs. Periwinkle hates him," Stinky said.

"Yes, good. That's one," Fernando replied.

"Magnus can't stand him," Thorin added.

"Yes, that's true." Fernando nodded.

"Todd, and Chip and Biff and Skip and . . ."

"Yes, very good, all the Algonquins hate him. I get it. Who else?"

Stinky thought and said, "Mr. Cramps was trying to kill him with the softball."

"Excellent point, Frank."

"Don't forget Mrs. Periwinkle's horse, Lucifer!" Thorin added excitedly.

"Very good, although I think we can cross him off the letter plot. Okay, I'm sure Rodney has at least a dozen more enemies we don't know about . . ."

"Hey!" I interrupted. They all looked at me. "My girlfriend just broke up with me. Listening to how many people hate me isn't helping."

"Well, *we* like you. Right, boys?"

"Yeah!" they replied in unison.

Fernando went on. "We'll do whatever it takes to solve this mystery. Right, boys?"

"Yeah!" they said again.

"Even if it puts us at great personal risk. Right, boys?"

The usually loud table went silent. Everyone seemed to be studying their forks and spoons with great interest. Fernando leaned across the table. "I'll run any risk. And I've already identified our first opportunity to investigate."

"What opportunity?" I asked.

"Feast your eyes on this." He handed me his perfumed letter.

Dear Fernando,

You're invited to my home to discuss your punishment over lunch Friday at 12 p.m. I hope lobster is fine with you. I look forward to seeing you then.

All the best,

Hagatha Periwinkle

"Sounds like you're in for a rough time," I observed. "I scrape mussels and you eat lobster."

Fernando smiled. "We all have our roles in life. But don't you see? This is just the chance we need."

"How's that?" I asked. The rest of the table moved in closer to hear him.

"I'm invited to Mrs. Periwinkle's house. She's the most likely culprit. Even if those other people hate you, they probably don't have access to outgoing camp mail."

"That's true," Stinky added excitedly. "Good thinking." Everyone at the table, including me, was beginning to like Fernando's plan. That is, except for Fernando. A look of disappointment came on his face.

"What's wrong?" I asked.

"I just realized that I have no idea what I would search for. She's probably destroyed your original letters by now."

Almost in unison, my cabinmates and I sat back dejectedly.

"Not necessarily!" Thorin shouted. We sprang forward again and leaned in closer to hear what he had to say. After all, the kid was pretty smart.

Thorin rose up and his eyes glazed over. "Think of Muad'Dib's poor father, done in by a traitor!"

The whole table sat back slowly. Smart, yes, but nuts.

"No," he continued. "Don't you see? Spies! And in this case, our spy would need samples of your handwriting. When Baron Vladimir Harkonnen infiltrated House Atreides with the Suk doctor Wellington Yueh—"

Fernando coughed and interrupted. "All right. Enough gibberish for a moment. I'm trying to focus . . ."

"Wait, he's making sense," I said.

"You're scaring me, Rathbone. You mean you understand all the Baron Whookahaka stuff?"

"Not that. The letters. If she's forging my handwriting to fool my parents and Jessica, she's probably held on to my letters to keep copying my handwriting. Brilliant, Thorin!" Thorin took an elaborate bow. "Of course, it won't be easy for you to go snooping around."

"True. A lady's attention rarely strays from Fernando. It will probably be impossible for me to slip away. We'll need another way in, and sadly, campers are rarely invited into the Periwinkle house. However, Alison did mention that she was invited next week to something they have every year called the Girls' Cotillion Dinner."

"So was Tabitha," I added. "She told me like it was some big deal—that only the most popular girls get invited."

Fernando continued. "Alison said there'd be ten or eleven girls going. The perfect number for someone to slip away and snoop and not get caught. Too bad none of us are girls, though."

"Hello, boys." A silky voice interrupted us. I spun around. Alison's red hair blew in my direction. Her hand held a fancy pink envelope similar to Fernando's. She looked at me teasingly and I noticed her eyes sparkle. "I think this belongs to you." She smiled, handing me the envelope.

A little confused, I took it and removed the letter.

"Read it out loud," Thorin pleaded.

I cleared my throat and began:

Dear Rodweena,

It was truly a pleasure meeting you the other night. I think you are just the kind of young lady to invite to the annual Girls' Cotillion Dinner next Friday evening at 7 p.m. I look forward to seeing you there.

Sincerely,

Mrs. Periwinkle

"Excellent. That's it!" Fernando said with a beaming smile. "Problem solved."

As the meaning of his words became clear to me, my face fell forward into my plate for the second time that morning.

Fernando patted me on the shoulder. "Come, my friend, it is time to leave. And think on the bright side."

"What's that?" I muttered into my eggs.

"At least you're one of the popular girls!"

Chapter 15

HIGH HEELS AND DEER GUTS

A couple of days later, I met Alison out in the woods, past the archery range. We had arranged to go over a few details before my big change into Rodweena. Stinky came along too and sat on a stump, itching himself.

"What is that stuff?" I asked Alison.

"It's called blush," she answered, rubbing some on the top of my hand.

"What does it do?"

"Rodney, it makes your cheeks look red, like you're blushing. Boys like it when girls blush."

"They do? I mean, we do?"

"Yes, you do." She examined my hand. "I guess this color will work. Now, the night of Mrs. Periwinkle's party, you're really going to have to clean your fingernails. Look at those cuticles!"

"What's a cuticle?"

She rolled her eyes and pulled out a bottle of perfume.

"Don't tell me I have to wear that, too," I groaned.

"No, this is for him." She turned and sprayed Stinky a few times.

"Hey!" he whined.

She ignored his protests and continued talking to me. "This plan of Fernando's has a long way to go."

"You're the one who volunteered to help me," I reminded her.

She continued like she hadn't heard me. "Listen, the night of the party I'll meet you here, where no one will see us, and I'll help you get dressed. I still have the wig and I borrowed some pretty high heels."

This whole plan was sounding more and more impossible—and way more embarrassing if I got caught. Nevertheless, I was committed now. Plus there was something reassuring about Alison. I watched as she arranged everything, like she had done this a hundred times before. I liked the way she didn't make a fuss about things.

The summer leaves rustled in the afternoon breeze. In the distance you could hear kids shouting down by the lake. It felt fun to be meeting secretly like this in the woods. Alison had picked the spot—the old stone chimney. It was a chimney left standing in the middle of a small clearing. I guess a cabin had once surrounded the chimney, but it was long gone.

"Some farmer and his family probably lived here in the olden days," Alison said.

"I bet *he* didn't have to wear high heels," I joked.

She gave me a big smile and our eyes met. A second later her cheeks turned bright red.

"Is that blush you're wearing?" I asked.

"No, Rodney." She sighed, looking down.

I realized I really liked her. I was in the middle of admiring her long red hair and tan skin when she glanced up. Her deep brown eyes looked into mine. I gazed into them, starting to feel . . .

"Buuuurrrrrppp!" Stinky exploded.

Spell broken, Alison said, "Okay, I'm going to be late for windsurfing. Rodney, practice walking on your toes, with your hand on your hip. That will help you get ready for the high heels."

"Uh, all right. Thanks, I guess."

"Bye, Rodney. Bye, Frank."

"Bye, Alison," Stinky called.

I watched her walk down the path toward the lake. She rounded a bend in the trail and was gone. I stood for a second breathing in the warm, woodsy air. For the first time in a couple of days, my stomach wasn't in a knot over the sadness with Jessica.

Stinky and I turned and walked off in the other direction. I had athletics with Mr. Cramps. In no rush to do my usual assortment of push-ups, crunches, squat thrusts, and mile run, we took the longcut along a trail that followed a small creek. After a while I decided to practice walking on my tippy-toes. "Does it look like I'm walking like a girl?" I laughed.

Stinky answered, "I'm not sure. You *do* look pretty weird."

I tried a few more times. Then I put my hand on my hip, like Alison said. "How about now?"

"Get a load of this guy!"

It wasn't Stinky's voice. I spun around. Now, I've faced some pretty bad situations in my life, so I can't say I was completely surprised to see Todd and his usual pack of Algonquins. They were sitting on a log off the trail.

"Nice walk, Rathbone," Todd shouted, getting up. The Algonquins laughed and all rose off the log, starting to walk in our direction. Todd was actually wearing white pants and a white shirt. His hair shimmered in the sun.

"Nice outfit," I said. "I'll take a snow cone."

He wasn't amused. "So this is what you losers do for fun? Walk around like girls? Let me try." With that, he began to walk crazily down the path. "Look at *meee*. I'm Rod-*neee!* Whoop-*eee!*" The other Algonquins were laughing. Todd kept going, "La la—*ow!*" He stopped short and rubbed his forehead. "That hurt! What was that?" He reached down and picked up an acorn. "Did you throw this at me, Rathbone?"

I hadn't thrown anything. "Maybe the sky is falling."

"You're dead."

"Relax," I said, "we didn't do anything. Right, Frank?" There was no reply. I glanced over at him. "Right?"

Stinky shrugged. "Seemed like the thing to do at the time."

I couldn't believe it! Here, in the middle of the woods, Stinky suddenly decided to act brave. While I understood his logic, I also knew what would come next.

"Open fire!" Todd shouted. Within seconds, acorns whizzed through the air. I felt sharp stings on my shoulder and back. I scrambled behind a tree and looked for ammunition. Stinky was already launching acorns as fast as he could and I heard a couple of yelps from the Algonquins.

We put up a good fight that day, but as the battle wore on it was obvious we were outnumbered. My body stung in a dozen places where the acorns hit their marks. Todd threw an enormous acorn that zipped past my head and bounced off the tree with a loud whack. I knew I couldn't stay trapped behind the tree forever. I ran a few feet, jumped over the small, muddy creek, and turned and nailed Skip in the neck. As Stinky jumped over the stream to join me he let out a yell. A rock had left Todd's hand and hit him on the elbow. Stinky grabbed it and grimaced in pain. Todd wasn't playing by the rules.

"Hey, no rocks!" I yelled angrily.

Todd laughed. "Or else what? You going to tell your mommy?"

The last thing I wanted was a fight, but I was sick

of Todd thinking he could bully me. I looked around. "Come over here and I'll show you what I'll do!"

Todd smiled. "This ought to be interesting."

He took a few steps closer and was just on the other side of the stream when I made my move. "Hey, your shoelace is untied."

"Is that all you've got, Rathbone?" he laughed, turning to smile at his fellow Algonquins.

"Yeah . . . and THIS!"

In front of me were some large rocks. With two hands I grabbed one that weighed about forty pounds and heaved it into the creek. By the time Todd realized what I was doing it was too late. My boulder landed and sent up a wall of mud that covered him from head to foot, white pants and all. I locked eyes with Stinky. "Run!"

We spun around and took off, not on the path but straight into the woods. "You're dead!" Todd screamed, bounding after me like a madman. Small branches scraped and scratched my face but I kept running. Stinky got blocked by some thick underbrush and ran off in another direction. Unfortunately, there was no shaking Todd. As he closed in on me, I realized that maybe the mud thing hadn't been such a bright idea.

I ran a few more steps, suddenly finding myself on a rock ledge with nowhere to go. I think Todd tried to stop but it was too late. He smashed into me and we both flew through the air before dropping hard to the ground. My ankle twisted awkwardly when I landed. I tried to stand and balance on one foot, bracing for the punch that was surely coming my way. I could hear the other Algonquins, and hopefully Stinky, scrambling down the ledge. Todd said, "Now you're dea—"

He didn't finish. Something shut him up. I followed his gaze. A deer's head was hanging from a tree. Todd jumped and actually grabbed my shoulder. I followed his gaze. Several ratlike animals were nailed to another tree. We both gulped and looked further into the woods. Standing with the sun behind him, so that we could only see his dark outline, was a large man dressed for a horror movie audition moving closer.

I turned, trying to run, but pain shot from my ankle and I stumbled to the ground. Not surprisingly, Todd didn't pause to help me up. He was too busy tearing off at full speed, following everyone else. I watched, helpless, as he walked toward me. This was really it. Less than a half hour ago I was worried about high heels. Now I was about to die like some character in a bad horror movie.

"Yo Rodney," the guy greeted me. "You finally came out to my shack for that arrow shooting lesson. Good timing, too. I just cut out some deer kidneys. I'm frying them up right now for a snack."

It was Survival Steve, and I wasn't dead. In fact, he helped me up and almost lifted me over to his shack. He went in and came back out, handing me a tin plate. "Dig in!"

To be polite, I gagged some down. They were still kind of raw and disgusting, but at that moment I was so relieved not to be up in the tree with the deer head that I'd have eaten dog doo.

"Guess you could use a drink, too," he said as I sat on a stool, wiping deer blood from my chin. "Let's see, I got some two day old coffee, some goat pee, some . . ."

"I'm fine, thanks. The kidneys hit the spot."

"Yeah, they do, don't they? Now let's go shoot some arrows." I stood to follow him and winced. He looked down at my ankle.

"Well now, that's something, ain't it? No matter, got just the thing." In no time he had pulled out some sticks and rawhide rope and was weaving me a splint. He talked while he worked. "I was attacked by a moose up in Alaska one spring. Almost broke my legs in two. I fashioned myself some leg braces and walked two hundred miles to Anchorage . . ."

"Sounds like a nice vacation," I quipped.

"The best," he agreed. "Now, stand up."

It was amazing. Somehow the splint thing took almost all the pressure off my ankle. I walked around. "I can't believe you figured this out using just your survival instincts."

"Yeah, that and a degree in orthopedics from Johns Hopkins." I glanced up at him. He continued, "Hey, are we going to shoot arrows or what?"

Steve lived up to his promise and for the next couple

of hours we shot arrows at a big old stump. He showed me how to hold a bow and how to control my arm's motion. I couldn't believe it, but I was pretty good. I hit the target again and again. After I hit the same small spot fourteen times in a row, Steve howled enthusiastically, "You're a natural, Rodney!"

"This is a lot of fun," I answered.

"You bet, but it'll be dinnertime back at camp soon. Your counselor will be wondering where you are."

I pictured Woo, head bopping, lost in his own jazz world. I doubted he would miss me. I was having a good time out at the shack. I said, "All right, but not before I shoot this arrow into that birch trunk down there."

"Way down yonder?" Steve asked.

"Yeah, down yonder." I smiled to myself, realizing I sounded like a hillbilly.

"That'd be some throw, I doubt—"

I didn't wait for his reply. I stepped in and let the arrow fly. It sailed straight and sweet and landed with a *thunk* right where I said it would go.

"Whooooeeeeeeee! Come back next week and I'll teach you how to wrestle a bear. All right, let's go. I'll help you back. Oh, here."

"What's this?" I looked down at something wrapped in wax paper.

"It's another deer kidney. I know how you like 'em."

"Mmm, dessert," I said, holding it up.

We walked back through the woods. Along the way Steve pointed out different streams, climbing trees, caves, and even the entrance to an old mine.

"Where does that go?"

"Well, if you stay to the right in the mine, you'll wind up down by the lake, near the boys' cabins. Dangerous place, though. Stay out of it."

Eventually, we neared camp. I could see the dining hall through the trees. "Guess you can manage from here," Steve said.

I smiled, said thanks and good-bye, and walked up the hill to the dining hall. Everyone was lined up waiting to go in, and I thought I heard my name mentioned a few times. Mr. Periwinkle was busy questioning Woo, who was staring off singing, "Nothing's gonna bring him back." Seeing me emerge from the woods, my cabinmates let out a shout and came running.

"Glad you made it!" Stinky yelled.

"Piece of cake," I said, smiling.

"I didn't know what to do," Stinky continued. "I tried to get help, but when I got out of the woods, Magnus told me to be quiet and sent me back to the cabin."

Todd and the Algonquins had also walked my way. "I thought you were dead," Todd said. I noticed he had changed into clean clothes.

"Sorry to disappoint you. Oh, here's a souvenir. I kind of tore it out of that guy while we were fighting."

I tossed him the now-unwrapped deer kidney. He caught it, looked down, and screamed, "Whoooaaahhh!"

I laughed. And then, along with my friends, I headed into the dining hall, where over a fine dinner of dry meatloaf, lumpy mashed potatoes, smelly green beans, and a cup of red bug juice, I related my adventures.

Chapter 16

RODWEENA'S NIGHT OUT

Alison and Fernando helped me stumble out from the woods where I had climbed into my Rodweena outfit.

"My, my, Rodney, you look . . ."

"Zip it, Fernando. I'll give this crazy plan of yours a shot, but I don't have to like it." Both of their eyes were sparkling, and I could tell they were really enjoying seeing me grumble about being dressed like a girl. "Do you think this is going to work?" I asked.

Fernando and Alison looked at me closer. Fernando said, "You'd better stay out of the kitchen."

"Why, does this outfit make me look fat?"

"No, the bright lights will give you away. Keep to the shadows. I don't know how long it will take, but someone will probably realize you're not a girl. And if that happens, I'm glad Fernando won't be there to see what Mrs. Periwinkle does to you."

I tried to block that frightening thought as I

concentrated on the task at hand. My time would be limited. I had to act fast and get out before getting caught. Get in, get out.

"Remember, the office is down the hall to the right," Fernando continued. "If she has your letters, that's where you'll probably find them." I nodded. Fernando had done some preliminary scouting during his punishment luncheon of chilled lobster and chocolate-covered strawberries. "All right, good luck, girls!" he called with a laugh as he turned and headed off.

Alison and I walked up the steep hill leading to the Periwinkles' house. It was a nice night, with fireflies flashing everywhere and a million stars overhead. I took a second to sneak a glance at her. At least one of us was looking good tonight. Funny, I hadn't really paid much attention to Alison when I first got to camp, but now . . .

Arriving at the house, she fixed the wig on my head and said, "Remember, tonight you're a girl. Act like one." Before I had a chance to run, she knocked.

A moment later the door opened and I could see Mrs. Periwinkle standing behind the screen. Her eyes lingered on me for a few torturous seconds. Was I caught already? Then she smiled. "Oh, Rodweena, so nice to see you. You look very . . . uh . . . pretty. What an interesting hairstyle you're wearing. Hello, Alison. That's a very nice dress." This was definitely a different Mrs. Periwinkle than the one who cursed me under her breath every time she saw me. "Come in, come in," she continued. "The girls are all out back. Just make your way straight through the house."

I was feeling nervous as I passed her so I kept my head down and speed-walked my way through the living and dining rooms.

"Rodney," Alison whispered from over my shoulder, "you're stomping around like a soldier. Remember, you're a girl."

"Oh, yeah. I'll remember. Thanks." I felt like I was going to get caught any minute. Mrs. Periwinkle was right behind us in the hallway. I don't know if it was my nerves or all the bug juice I drank at lunch, but suddenly I had to go to the bathroom real bad. "Mrs. Periwinkle," I asked in my highest voice, "may I use the restroom?"

"It's just through the kitchen," she replied.

The kitchen! I braved the bright lights and crossed to the bathroom door. Once inside, I turned the lock, exhaled, and stood there taking care of my business. When finished, I actually felt a little better. "Remember, act like a girl," I said to myself in the mirror. "And remember to get in and get out. No small talk with anyone. Don't even stay for dinner." I opened the door and walked smack into Mrs. Periwinkle. "Oh, excuse me."

"Careful, Rodweena." She stepped past me and headed into the bathroom. "I'll be just a minute."

The lock clicked and so did my brain. Get in, get out! I could go to the office right now, find the letters, and be out into the night. I glanced back and forth. Which way?

"AAAAAAAAEEEEEEEEEAAAAAAAAHHH-HHH!" A howl exploded from behind the closed door. What happened? I heard more grunts, angry snorts, and banging. I had just decided to run for it when the door swung open. Mrs. Periwinkle's dress was wet and twisted and she looked even crazier than usual. In a loud, clipped breath she said, "Rodweena, why on earth did you *PUT THE SEAT UP?*"

Oh no! I was pretending to be a girl and I did the one thing no girl would ever do. My mom always yelled at me for that.

"Well, I, uh . . ."

"I was momentarily stuck!" she howled. "I could have drowned! And look what you did to my beautiful evening gown."

Mrs. Periwinkle adjusted her outfit. The pause allowed my brain to kick into gear. Remembering something my great aunt Evelyn usually said, I offered, "But Mrs. Periwinkle, I didn't use the toilet. I was just powdering my nose."

Her sneer lost its ferocity. I tried to look sincere and she softened more. "Well, I guess that makes sense. It is always smart for a young lady to check herself before entering a social gathering. Well done, Rodweena. But if *you* didn't put the seat up . . ." Her face looked thoughtful and then suddenly furious. "PERCY!"

From somewhere above I heard a startled jump, and then silence. Mrs. Periwinkle gazed at the ceiling, her eyes blazing once again. After a minute of huffing, she looked back down and said, "I'll deal with him later. Let's go enjoy the night."

After our rather eventful trip to the john, we walked outside. Before me I saw three tables covered with white linen. Fireflies flew between pink and yellow Chinese lanterns suspended from several old oak trees that surrounded the back patio. Soft music played. I had to admit, it was very nice.

Alison was already sitting at a table under the largest of the oak trees. I headed in her direction, but Mrs. Periwinkle stopped me. "Rodweena, I feel positively awful about what just happened. Come sit at my table."

"But . . ."

"There are no buts about it. I insist. You shall be the guest of honor. You know, I was very impressed with you the other night and I want to talk further."

"Sounds wonderful, Mrs. Periwinkle," I lied. The last thing I wanted was to be stuck with her. I'd be found out for sure, and any chance of slipping away would be very small.

She motioned to the table that had the best view overlooking the camp fields. As I stood there awkwardly, stalling so I didn't have to sit, I realized that the whole plan was dumb. I wanted to get out of there. It was pointless anyway. The chance of finding the letters was slim, and if I ran off before getting caught nothing bad would happen. No one knew who I *really* was, anyway.

I was just turning to leave when I noticed who was seated at Mrs. Periwinkle's table.

Tabitha was wearing a light-green dress that matched her eyes. They glowed more wonderfully than any of the fireflies or lanterns. I stumbled as I ran to take the seat next to her, banging my knee into the table leg. *Get in, get out* was suddenly replaced by. *Be cool, act cool.* I placed the napkin in my lap and gave her a wink.

She made a weird face and I remembered who I was—or, perhaps more appropriately, who I wasn't. "Oh, a mosquito flew into my eye," I said, rubbing it. Tabitha seemed to accept this. I looked around at the other girls. I recognized some but didn't really know them. So far Alison was the only girl there who knew my real identity. I noticed that she was looking at me from the other table—and she didn't look happy. Was it because I was sitting next to Tabitha?

Mrs. Periwinkle stood behind her seat, cleared her throat, and announced, "Young ladies, I'm delighted you could all join me tonight for the annual Girls' Cotillion Dinner." She beamed at us. "Cotillions are traditionally gatherings where young people learn the manners of polite society. It's important to have a few moments like this, away from the dining hall with its often loud and raucous behavior. Tonight we can engage in refined conversation, practice proper etiquette, and talk about subjects young ladies find interesting." Boy, was this boring. I wished I was in the *dining* hall. "Also, I have made sure that we have an excellent menu tonight . . ."

What's that? It was then that I noticed some waiters and a catering van parked below us in the driveway. *Let's hear it for cotillions!* I thought.

"Tonight we'll be partaking of shrimp cocktail, Caesar salad, lobster bisque, and filet mignon. Nothing is too fine or expensive for you young ladies. After all, I'll soon be coming into quite a bit of . . ."

She seemed to think better of continuing, but we all knew she was about to say "money." I didn't really care. I was too busy drooling and trying to quiet my growling stomach. After weeks of Gertrude and Alice's cooking, McDonald's would have seemed like gourmet dining. My thoughts of making a quick escape faded as I contemplated a mouthwatering steak. Mrs. Periwinkle concluded, "I hope you enjoy."

She sat down and smiled at the table. "All right, girls, I've really been looking forward to tonight. Sometimes one needs to spend time with just the girls. Don't you agree, Rodweena?"

"Oh, I agree, Mrs. Periwinkle. A night away from boys is like an oasis in the desert." I could tell she liked that one. Her face beamed with warmth. It went cold, however, following a loud crash from inside the house.

"Who's in there?" she snapped loudly.

Mr. Periwinkle's face slowly rose into view through the kitchen window.

"What are you doing?" she growled.

"I was just making a sandwich. I dropped the mayo ..."

"*Get back to your room!*" There was another bang as we heard him scurry away. Mrs. Periwinkle exhaled slowly. "Yes, Rodweena, an oasis."

A waiter placed a tall glass with three large shrimp in front of me. I almost elbowed Tabitha out of excitement. I licked my lips, grabbed a shrimp, dipped it in the cocktail sauce and opened my mouth to take a bite.

"So, Rodweena, the other night you made so much sense and had such strong convictions. What would you like to talk about tonight?" Everyone turned to me expectantly.

I lowered the shrimp. "Well, I wonder who's going to win the AFC East this fall. I like the Jets, and I can't stand the Patriots, but with their quarterback ..." The collection of female faces looked surprised—and disgusted. I came close to smacking my forehead. I gathered myself and gave a big laugh. "Baseball! Hah! Can you believe boys waste their time talking about such nonsense? I'd love to talk about jewelry. That's a nice necklace thing, Mrs. Periwinkle." Their faces relaxed.

Mrs. Periwinkle smiled and I went to bite the shrimp.

"Rodweena," she continued. I lowered the shrimp. "I thought we might want to talk about the many fine young gentlemen around camp." A couple of girls giggled. *Okay*, I thought to myself. *You talk about what-ever. I'm going to finally eat this shrimp.*

It was halfway to my mouth when Mrs. Periwinkle said my name again. "Rodweena, I bet you and young Todd Vanderdick would make a darling couple . . ."

"What?" I shouted, forgetting to disguise my voice.

Mrs. Perwinkle seemed to study me a bit closer. Was I caught? I put the shrimp back down and added, in a more girl-like voice, "Why, whatever gave you that idea?"

"Oh, *everyone* likes Todd. Isn't that true, Tabitha?" Tabitha stirred in her seat and smiled slyly. Mrs. Periwinkle sure seemed to be enjoying herself.

I could feel my mouth getting tingly, and I said, "Tabitha, I thought you liked Rodney Rathbone?"

Mrs. Periwinkle recoiled. "Rodweena, just *hearing* that name gives me indigestion. Let's not spoil a lovely evening. Surely Tabitha has more taste than to give that horrible boy any thought. Am I right, Tabitha?"

"Absolutely, Mrs. Periwinkle."

I felt a little anger smoldering, but I did my best to hide it and decided to finally eat my shrimp. Just as I reached for one, the waiter whisked the three juicy beauties away and replaced them with the salad. I almost cried. With a growling stomach I took a bite and discovered that it was actually good. It had a tasty dressing and big, crunchy croutons.

Not everyone agreed with me. "Where are the

anchovies?" We all looked up at Mrs. Periwinkle, who was rooting around her salad with her fork. "I distinctly requested anchovies in the Caesar." I looked down fearfully, afraid that I might find slimy bits of fish hiding between my lettuce leaves. "Unacceptable!" Mrs. Periwinkle dropped her napkin on the table and stomped off in a huff after one of the waiters.

Tabitha leaned in to me and asked, "Rodweena, who told you that I like Rodney? I've never even seen you before." I was stuck, but before I could make up an answer she added, "And why are you bringing him up around Mrs. Periwinkle? She can't stand him."

"Oh, sorry. Anyway, I just assumed you liked him. I didn't know you didn't."

"Who says I don't?"

"Well, you just did . . ."

Tabitha smiled and said in a quiet breath, "Don't be silly, Rodweena. I do like Rodney. I think he's a bad boy. He's exciting."

I never thought of myself as an exciting bad boy before. Feeling pretty good, I asked, "So you don't like Todd, then?"

"No, I like him, too. He's got lots of money. Do you know his dad has a yacht?"

My good feelings died, but I asked, "So which are you going to . . . you know, date?"

"Both," she said, taking a bite of lettuce like it was nothing.

"Both? What if one of them finds out?"

"Rodweena, they're boys. *Clueless!* There's absolutely no chance either will find out."

"The odds might be higher than you think," I added. Tabitha laughed and shook her head at me like I was crazy, and then shifted her eyes upward to tell me Mrs. Periwinkle had returned.

The two of them were making me lose my appetite and I suddenly focused again on the reason for being here. I had to complete the mission.

"Excuse me, Mrs. Periwinkle. I need to use the bathroom."

"Well, you know where it is," she responded, followed by, "and make sure the seat is down."

I pretended to laugh at her little joke and rose from the table. As I passed Alison I gave her a subtle nod and continued into the house. It was now or never. *Get in, get out.*

Chapter 17

THE PLOT THICKENS

Instead of heading through the kitchen toward the bathroom, I turned left down a dimly lit hallway. I could see a faint green light shining under the door. If Fernando's description was accurate, my letters home would be in the private den.

I grasped the cold glass knob. My heart started to beat hard and fast. This was it. I could barely stand to watch detectives on TV when they might get caught, and now I was sneaking into an office. It felt strange, almost like I was watching someone else's hand twisting and pulling the knob. I entered and quickly closed the door behind me.

Knowing I had limited time, I dove right into the papers on the desk, looking for the letters. It was easy to see because someone had left on an old-fashioned desk lamp that gave off a weird green glow. The papers were only about some boring legal stuff, something about wetland development and parking lot design. I pushed them aside and looked through several folders. Again, nothing. I stole a glance and noticed one last folder with a red tab that read PSYCHOLOGICAL PROFILE— DANGEROUS CAMPER. That caught my attention. Was there some dangerous person lurking around Camp Wy-Mee? It'd be a good idea to know who I should avoid.

I looked for a name, but all that I could see was *Camper RR*. The next page had all the basic information, such as age, height, eye color, hair color. Other basic characteristics were listed. It could be anyone. Heck, it could be *me*. I read on:

> Hagatha, please remember that Camper RR must be watched at all times. On the surface he appears normal enough, but don't let that fool you. His mind is constantly working out dangerous, evil plots. Making him even more of a threat is his knack for emboldening the usually quieter children. Some thick-headed adults are also captivated by his sickening charm . . .

Who wrote this thing? Who was Camper RR? My hand bumped against the mouse and the computer screen came to life. An icon on the screen flashed: "Urgent email." My curiosity got the better of me and I opened it. It read:

Hagatha, I'm disappointed you haven't taken care of our little problem by now. Must I handle everything? I'll be seeing you real soon. Love, Big Sis.

What was that about? Could it be about Camper RR? About me? And who was Mrs. Periwinkle's big sister? I turned my attention back to the matter at hand. I had been snooping around the office for two minutes and would soon be missed. It was then that I noticed the corner of two white envelopes sticking out from under a book. My heart started to beat even faster. The envelopes looked just like the ones my mom had given me before camp so I could write home. This was it. I reached out and started to lift the book. Then I saw the phone and another idea jumped into my brain.

While everyone else had been allowed to use the camp phone once a week after dinner, my privileges had been suspended. And now there it was, a phone just waiting for me. Before I had time to think, I reached into my wallet, took out a piece of paper with a number scribbled on it, and called Jessica.

"Hello."

It was her voice. My heart beat hard. "Hi, Jessica. It's Rodney."

"Rodney? I didn't think I'd hear from you after that terrible letter you sent..."

"Jessica, I didn't write that letter. I know it sounds crazy, but someone's been intercepting my mail—"

"You're right, it does sound crazy. Now I need to go."

"Don't hang up, Jessica. Why would I break up with you? I spent the entire year trying to get you to like me. You're the coolest, prettiest, best girl in Ohio . . ."

"Do you really think so?"

"Absolutely! I would never write horrible things to you."

"It really hurt my feelings."

"Jessica, I'm sorry that happened to you. I want you to know that I would never do anything mean or rude or—"

I smacked down the receiver. The doorknob was beginning to turn. There was a closet on the other side of the room. I wouldn't make it in time. Instead, I jumped behind the curtains as the door opened and closed.

From my hiding spot I couldn't see who had entered the room, but I was sure that whoever it was could see me shaking like a leaf behind the curtain.

"Hello, Bill. It's Percy." Mr. Periwinkle must have come into the office to use the phone. He was whispering and talking very fast. "Hagatha is having a girls' dinner here so I can only talk a second. I wanted you to know that I got your message and I think it's great. Endangered salamanders might be our last chance to save this place. If that doesn't work, Hagatha and her battle-ax sister will have their way for sure. I know their plan will make us all rich, but these woods are worth far more to me. Of course, I only have a slight say in the matter . . ." His voice seemed to trail off. "Thank you for trying, Bill. We'll talk more tomorrow."

After a moment I heard the door close. Peeking out from behind the curtain, I checked that the coast was clear and ran over to the desk. I could still hear Periwinkle walking about and I knew time was running short. I pulled the two envelopes out from under the book—and stood looking down at my own handwriting. Mrs. Periwinkle really had intercepted my mail!

For a moment I debated whether to take the letters, but in the end I left both. I wanted to talk to Fernando before I did anything. I needed to figure it all out. What kind of person kept secret files on campers? What kind of person forged a kid's letter to his parents? And why was Mr. Perwinkle talking about salamanders?

It was time for me to get out of here. I slid open the window facing the woods, lowered myself down, and ran off to the dining hall, where I ditched my Rodweena costume under the steps. It felt good to be dressed like myself again. It wasn't until I was back in my bunk that I remembered the worst part about the night. I had hung up on Jessica and didn't even call her back! Imagining her reaction to my bonehead move was harder to digest than Mrs. Periwinkle's nonexistent anchovies.

Chapter 18

MY SPECIAL VISITOR

I was shaken awake early. Thorin, Josh, Fernando, and Stinky were all standing over me. "Well?" they asked.

I sat up and told them the details of what I had read and heard in the Periwinkles' office. Everyone listened carefully—even Josh. When I finished, Fernando let out a slow, quiet whistle and Thorin said, "It reminds me of the plots of Morgan le Fay."

As usual, Thorin was met with a round of blank stares. And as usual, he didn't notice. "Perhaps, Rodney," he continued, "she sees you as Arthur Pendragon."

"And perhaps you could join us on Earth," Fernando suggested. "Now, we need to figure some things out. We know Mrs. Periwinkle intercepted the mail, but we don't know why. We know she and this big sister of hers are plotting something against the camp. But we don't know what. Gentlemen, there are questions that need answers. We must go out there focused"—he pointed to the door—"and keep our eyes open."

"And our ears," Stinky added.

"Yes, Frank, and our ears."

"And our elbows," Josh added.

"Uh, okay, right."

BLLLLLAAAAAAAAAAAAAAAAAAAAAAAHH-HHHHHHHH! A siren wailed so loudly that it actually shook the cabin's frame. It sounded like it was blaring all over camp.

Stinky screamed, "It's Mrs. Periwinkle! She's bombing us!" and went scurrying under his bunk bed. Thorin grabbed Orcrist and held it ready to strike any goblin that should appear. Josh lifted his trunk high over his head and stood there grinning, caught up in the excitement.

"No time for da nerves, everyone," Woo announced as the siren slowly came to an end. "It's Secret Special Visitors Day. Let's go play. Whaddaya say?"

Josh looked disappointed as he lowered his trunk, but the rest of us were relieved. After he climbed out from under his bunk, Stinky remembered what the whistle meant. It seemed that Secret Special Visitors Day was a yearly event. The campers never knew when it was coming and enjoyed being surprised by their family members. I was a little skeptical.

"*Everyone* has a visitor?" I asked. "I mean, what if someone can't make it?"

"No," Stinky explained. "They almost always have one hundred percent attendance. It's written into the

Camp Wy-Mee application or something. It's manda-
tory. Mr. Periwinkle thinks it's a big deal and insists on
it. Anyway, the day's great. There are fun activities and
there'll be a big barbecue tonight!"

"So when do we see our visitors?" I was starting to
get excited. "I can't wait!"

Woo said, "Don't be impatient, don't you whine,
your visitors will be there, now get in line." He strutted
toward the door.

Josh was the first to follow him. Woo turned back to
him, smiling. "Come on, Joshy. I know you got the gift.
You're the Knick with the knack, so rap, rap, rap. Give
me a rhyme while there's still some time."

Josh was lost. If his jaw hung any lower, it would
have dragged on the floor.

"Just say a word, Josh." Woo smiled. "Any word."

Josh, who was about to step outside, looked down
and managed to utter, "Stair."

"Yeah, man! No sittin' in the *chair*. Keep breathing
the *air*. Why should you *care*? Drag that comb through
your . . ." Woo pointed at Josh.

Miraculously, Josh uttered, "Hair."

"SNAP!" Woo clapped his hands together. "My car
has a *spare*. My favorite fruit is a *pear*. I like to watch the
Fresh Prince of *Bel-Air*. When I drum I use a *snare*. In
the woods I tracked a . . ."

"Wolf!" Josh exclaimed proudly. He held up his hand
to high-five Woo.

For once, Woo was at a loss for words. He dumbly tapped Josh's hand.

I pushed past them with Fernando and wandered over to the line. Since last night, my head had been consumed with evil plots and conspiracies. Now, with the knowledge that in ten minutes I'd be seeing a family member, my worries faded. Who was it? My brain ran through the possibilities. According to the letter I had received, my parents were away on vacation. And then it came to me . . . the one relative who'd be more than willing to head off to camp for a day of fun. Aunt Evelyn! I was all smiles as we walked the familiar path to the dining hall.

As we approached, I watched the girls walking from the other direction and I could hear a steady hum of conversation pouring out from the dining hall windows. Who was in there waiting for me?

We still had to line up and do the usual flag-raising and singing ceremonies. During "America the Beautiful" I made eye contact with Alison. I could see that she was itching to find out about the rest of my night. I, too, wanted to hear what commotion Rodweena's disappearance had caused.

The singing ended and Mr. Periwinkle climbed on top of the announcement boulder, waiting for us to quiet down. I noticed he wore his special-occasion pith helmet.

"May I have your attention? I realize you're excited,

but a few words first. Right now your visitors are seated in the dining hall. After you have brunch with them, there are numerous activities arranged for you to enjoy together. It should be a splendid afternoon. Tonight we will finish the day with the annual camp barbecue—and *I'll* be manning the grill. Oh yes, one more thing." Suddenly Mr. Periwinkle looked right at me. "Rodney and Todd, may I see you for a moment? Everyone else, off you go."

The crowd stampeded toward the dining hall like a herd of hungry cattle. I wandered over to Mr. Periwinkle. What did he want to talk to me about? Was he going to tell me that I didn't have a visitor? Had he found out about Rodweena and that I went through his desk? If so, why was Todd there? Maybe he was going to ask Todd to beat me up. I didn't like this one bit.

Todd and I reached him at about the same moment. Todd's eyes gave me a nasty squint, and we turned to Periwinkle. Up close, despite his fancy helmet, I could see that Mr. Periwinkle looked jumpy and nervous. "Okay then," he began. "I asked to talk to you two because your special visitors are not in the dining hall." My heart dropped into my gut. I *knew* no one was going to visit me. "They are up at my house." My heart leaped back up into my chest. "We'll be dining there this morning."

Todd smirked, "Did Dad bring me anything?"

"I'm sure he did."

"Who's *my* special visitor?" I asked.

"Well, Rodney, I can't tell you that. She insisted that it remain a surprise." Looking back on it, I remember his voice sounded strained as he said this, but at that moment my brain was focusing on "she." It *had* to be my great-aunt Evelyn! She could charm a person in seconds and Mrs. Periwinkle must have asked her up to the house. Aunt Evelyn would know what to do about all the problems and how to save the camp. The rest of the summer was going to be a breeze! I was so happy I called out, "Come on, Todd, old buddy! I'll race you to the top of the hill." He just looked disgusted and trudged along behind me with Mr. Periwinkle.

I was way ahead of them as I weaved through the old oak trees from last night and crossed the patio. I knocked on the same screen door where Mrs. Periwinkle had greeted Alison and me—I mean Rodweena—just hours earlier. Mrs. Periwinkle's voice called out, "Come in, Rodney."

As I turned in to the living room I saw Mrs. Periwinkle, who was in a chair facing me. She lifted her head and smiled. She was talking to someone across from her. The person's face was blocked by the chair's high back. I yelled, "Aunt Evelyn!" and ran around to the front of the chair.

It wasn't Aunt Evelyn.

It was someone I knew real well, though. If spending the day with my aunt was going to be a dream, the dream had instantly become something so terrible that the word *nightmare* wasn't even strong enough. For sitting there, with an evil smile playing around her gray, ugly lips, was my greatest enemy—an enemy who made Todd, Magnus, and Mr. Cramps look like a group of Care Bears. It was Mrs. Lutzkraut, my former teacher.

I thought I'd escaped her evil plots when the school year ended, but seeing her sitting there smiling her wicked grin I knew I was in trouble. She was the nastiest person I knew, my greatest adversary, and I was a long way from home.

Chapter 19

THE MILLION-DOLLAR BET

"Did you miss me, Rodney?"

I felt dizzy. My heart was still beating fast from the run up the hill—and now this. I couldn't answer. I couldn't even think.

Mrs. Lutzkraut lifted a teacup and took a noisy sip. "Come now, Rodney. I'm disappointed. That famous mouth of yours has nothing to say?"

"Uhhhh..." I thought I was going to be sick. "What? Who? Uhhh..." Nonsense poured out from my mouth.

"I see that intelligent conversation is still light-years beyond you. I was hoping the camp air might have done you some good. Tell me, Rodney, are you enjoying your summer?" That famous wicked smile wouldn't leave her face and I could tell she was now enjoying *her* summer to the fullest. My brain began to piece things together.

"You're Mrs. Periwinkle's older sister?"

Mrs. Lutzkraut almost spit out her tea. "We prefer

'big sister'," she corrected me. "Anyway, that's a fine deduction. Apparently my efforts teaching you this past year weren't a complete waste." She reached into a bowl of chocolates on the coffee table. As I watched her pick at the silver foil surrounding each candy my brain began to kick into gear. Of course! *She* was probably the one who had told Mrs. Periwinkle to steal my mail.

"So tell me," she continued, picking some chocolate from her teeth with a finger nail, "How has Josh Dumbrowski been treating you?" Her smile gained a little ferocity. No doubt, she thought he was giving me a hard time.

"Good," I answered. "We're great pals now. Thank you for getting us together."

The side of her face twitched for a second. "It looks like you're having yourself a very nice little summer." I thought I caught a swift, nasty glance aimed at her sister. "*Too* nice a summer."

Mrs. Periwinkle added defensively, "Helga, I did everything you asked of me. I even—"

"Silence!"

We both jumped. Mrs. Lutzkraut regained her composure before continuing. "Rodney, I saw your friend Jessica in Garrettsville. She looked very happy. She was walking with some tall, handsome lad. I think he's a quarterback."

That one hurt. Mrs. Lutzkraut saw it on my face and her eyes twinkled. She stood up and walked over to the window. After a minute she motioned for me to join her. I glanced around nervously, but decided to do what she wanted.

"Rodney, look out there and tell me what you see."

I gazed out the large bay window. The fields and woods stretched out before us. The trees seemed to go on for miles. "Woods," I answered.

"That's right, Rodney. Woods. Deep, dark woods. Woods that can be a very perilous place for an unsuspecting young person . . ."

Still nuttier than a fruitcake, I thought to myself, remembering one of my dad's favorite expressions.

"There are no parents in the woods," she continued, "and no *Mr. Feebletops.*" Her voice shook at the mention of my former principal, who had always been kind to me. "I want you to rest easy, though, Rodney. I want you to know that for the remainder of the summer, *I'll* be spending lots of time at Camp Wy-Mee. Do you know why?"

"Because they ran you out of Garrettsville?"

"No, smarty-pants. Because I own this camp with my sister and I want to make sure my former star student receives all the extra attention he deserves."

She gave me a gentle pat on the shoulder. Despite it being early August and close to 90 degrees, her touch turned my body to ice.

I was rather used to Mrs. Lutzkraut's veiled, evil threats, but this one made my heart miss a beat or two.

In the past, when I was a student in her class, I would return each afternoon to my nice, safe house. The fact that I was now in camp—a camp she apparently owned—made it a whole different ball game. Easily disguised disasters could befall me in a variety of ways, and with no parents for hundreds of miles, I was in deep . . .

EEEErrrrrrrrrrr!! I jumped as the screen door creaked open. Todd and Mr. Periwinkle walked in. "Where's my special visitor?" Todd demanded.

Mrs. Lutzkraut's whole look changed. A genuine smile replaced her snakelike expression, and she replied lightly, "Oh, your father is just out back. Hagatha, go tell Mr. Vanderdick that his son is here."

Mrs. Periwinkle went out the back door and Mr. Periwinkle began to follow. "Not so fast, Percy!" Mrs. Lutzkraut snapped. I looked over. Mr. Periwinkle had one foot out the door. "Now that I have you and Vanderdick in one place, we're going to finish this thing once and for all."

She seemed to have momentarily forgotten about Todd and me. I slid back into the shadows of the dining room, wondering what "this thing" was.

I didn't have to wait long. Mrs. Periwinkle returned, trailed by a man in a lime-green shirt, a blue belt with sailboats on it, and fancy-looking tan pants. I noticed that he was wearing leather shoes and pink socks. This had to be Mr. Vanderdick. He flashed a perfect smile as he engulfed Todd in a hug, his white teeth contrasting sharply with his dark, tan skin. Vanderdick released his son, peeled off his sunglasses, and turned to face the women in the room. "Helga, Hagatha, how are my two favorite sisters?"

Helga? It was the second time I'd heard Mrs. Lutzkraut's first name, but now, slightly removed from immediate harm, I had time to think about it. The first syllable sure made sense to me.

Mr. Vanderdick continued, "Are we ready to become even richer?"

Mrs. Lutzkraut, smiling, answered, "We most certainly are."

Snap! Vanderdick's fingers made a crisp, sharp sound. The back door creaked open and three guys in dark suits walked in carrying brown briefcases. Was this part of "the thing" Mrs. Lutzkraut had mentioned? My curiosity was aroused. I slid behind a chair, figuring she'd kick me out of the house if she saw me.

"I brought all the final paperwork," Vanderdick announced proudly. "Three signatures and Camp Wy-Mee becomes Wy-Mee Estates. Over a hundred townhouses surrounding the lake, four hundred time-share units where the cabins now stand, an eighteen-hole golf course and clubhouse, and, of course, the Wy-Mee Mega Mall. It will be the flagship property of Vanderdick Global Enterprises."

"What about the Applebee's, Dad?"

"Yes, Todd, we will build an Applebee's."

So *that's* what Mrs. Lutzkraut had meant! Vanderdick was a developer, of course. The camp was going to be bull-dozed over for a mall and some dumb houses. I thought of all the spots I had come to love—the woods, Steve's shack, the campfire pit, the lakefront. I realized it would all be chopped up, carved up, and messed up. A feeling of disgust rippled along my skin as I looked around at the faces of the people prepared to do this thing. Mr. Vanderdick and Mrs. Lutzkraut were beaming. The lawyers looked serious and blank. Todd gazed at his dad as if he were some conquering hero. Mrs. Periwinkle smiled, but seemed nervous. I followed her glance.

Mr. Periwinkle's whole body seemed to be sagging to the floor. He hugged his pith helmet tight to his chest and his eyes held the look of someone learning about the death of a loved one. And as I thought about it, he was.

Mr. Vanderdick spread the papers on the coffee table and pulled a gold pen from his chest pocket. He said, "Your lawyers have gone over all the particulars. Here are the three places to sign. As fifty percent owner of Camp Wy-Mee, Helga, you sign here." He handed her the pen and she signed without even reading a word. "Now," Vanderdick continued, "Hagatha and Percy, since you jointly own the other fifty percent, I will need both of your signatures to make this complete."

Mrs. Lutzkraut stared at Mr. Periwinkle. "Percy, come over here and sign the paper."

"I can't do it," he whimpered.

"*Percy* . . . ," Mrs. Lutzkraut growled in an icy tone. "We've gone over this a hundred times."

"I know, but I can't. I won't . . ."

Now it was Vanderdick's turn. "Listen, Percy, you know you're never going to get another offer like this. I bought up all the land surrounding the camp and I swear that I'll ruin the area for any other developer. Does the word *strip-mining* mean anything to you?"

Mrs. Lutzkraut took a step closer to her cowering brother-in-law and exploded. "You blithering idiot! Don't you realize how much money we could make? Millions and millions of dollars! And you're going to throw it all away over some trees and a frog or two? Why my sister married you I'll never know, and why my moron of a father gave you authority to block this deal I cannot imagine, but I will not have you ruin it!"

Mr. Periwinkle looked like he wanted to slide behind the chair with me, but he said again, "I won't sign the paper."

"AAAAAAAArrrrgghhhhhhhh!" Mrs. Lutzkraut was ready to rush at him. Then she turned to Vanderdick. "Isn't there some way we can still make this deal without him? I'll sell you my half right now."

"Helga, you know we can't. After your sister married Percy, your father specifically wrote it into the will that the camp could not be split up or sold without *everyone's* signatures. If you were to remarry, we would need *your* husband's signature as well."

I took a good look at Mrs. Lutzkraut and doubted they would ever need a fourth signature. Smoke seemed to shoot from her ears and nostrils. Then she screamed at her sister, "Why did you marry him? WHY?"

Mrs. Periwinkle looked confused and kind of sad. Her eyes went from her sister to Mr. Periwinkle. Before she had a chance to answer, Vanderdick motioned to the three guys in suits to leave. They immediately marched out the door in single file. In an instant, the fake smile vanished from Vanderdick's face and he turned toward Mr. Perwinkle. "Percy, when we went to Camp Wy-Mee together, I beat you in every competition. I beat you then and I'll beat you now. Some things never change, just like I know that Todd will be having his name carved in the totem pole as this year's canoe-race champion!"

"Well maybe this year the Cherokees will win!" Periwinkle snapped.

"Right. And maybe you'll grow a full head of hair!"

"That's it!" shouted Mr. Periwinkle, jamming the helmet onto his head and taking a step closer to Vanderdick. "You bullied me around all those years ago at camp, but I won't have you bully me in my own house. You want me to sign the papers? Fine, I'll sign them . . ."

A smile spread across Mrs. Lutzkraut's face.

"I will sign them," continued Mr. Periwinkle, "but under one condition . . ."

The room went silent. All eyes were on the man who, for the first time that day, was standing tall and proud. I almost shouted out, "What's the condition?" but I managed to keep my mouth shut.

"I will sign the agreement if, and only if, the Cherokees lose the end-of-summer canoe race."

I almost cheered this, but then I wondered what the canoe race was all about.

Mrs. Lutzkraut's smile snapped back to its usual sneer. "What's this nonsense you're mumbling about? Canoe race? We're talking about millions of dollars here and you're playing games."

Mr. Periwinkle turned and looked right at me. Mrs. Lutzkraut followed his gaze. Seeing me, she waved her hand at me in frustration. "I forgot you were here," she shouted. "It figures that this harebrained notion has something to do with you. What have you two cooked up?" I was curious, too. I had no idea how I had stumbled into the latest plot.

Mr. Periwinkle stepped forward. "Young Rodney here, and his Cherokee cabinmates, are my entrants in the canoe race. It's the oldest Camp Wy-Mee tradition. It dates back—"

"I know what it is, you nincompoop!" screamed Mrs. Lutzkraut. "My family's owned the camp for eighty years. I'm not basing millions on some camp competit—"

"If you want me to sign the agreement, you'll listen,

you . . . you . . ." He seemed to think better of finishing the sentence. He turned back to Vanderdick. "Rodney and his cabinmates will beat the Algonquin cabin. If Rodney's cabin wins, I don't have to sign the agreement and Camp Wy-Mee is left untouched—*and* you have to set up a land trust promising you won't develop any of the land adjoining Camp Wy-Mee you own. However, if the Algonquins win, I'll sign the papers. What do you say?"

I think you're crazy, I thought.

"I think you're crazy!" Lutzkraut yelled, actually scaring me, since it was the first time I had ever agreed with her. She continued, "You think I'm going to let Rodney Rathbone decide my fate? He cheats. He's a scoundrel. He's . . ."

"A loser," Todd interrupted.

"What?" Mrs. Lutzkraut asked, whirling around to face him.

"Look at him, the way he dresses, the way he acts, the kids he hangs out with. He's a born loser. The canoe race is a grueling two-day event. We'll have a blizzard in August before that kids beats me."

Mrs. Lutzkraut rubbed her chin. "Hmmmmmm."

"I am the camp's best canoer," Todd continued. "With Skip beside me, we'll win by ten miles. Mrs. Lutzkraut, Mrs. Periwinkle, Dad—the money is in the bag!"

Mr. Vanderdick puffed out his chest. The sisters looked thoughtful. I felt sick. Todd was right. There was no way I was going to win a canoe race.

"I won the canoe race three times when I was an Algonquin." Mr. Vanderdick laughed. "Remember, Percy? You were always so mad at us. How many years have the Algonquins won in a row?"

"Um, about twenty-two," Mr. Periwinkle said.

Todd looked up at his dad. "Soon to be twenty-three. No way we lose. We're going to pound that bunch of losers!"

"That's my boy," Vanderdick said, tousling his son's head. Then he pointed at me. "By the way, what cabin are you again?"

"Cherokee," I answered.

"Loserville?" Vanderdick laughed. I wanted to kick him in the shin. He looked over at Mr. Periwinkle. "No wonder you've got a soft spot for this kid. I seem to remember you were a permanent resident of Loserville. How many times, exactly, has that cabin won the canoe race?"

"Zero," Mr. Periwinkle said flatly.

The more I listened, the nuttier the whole thing sounded. Why was Periwinkle doing this?

Mr. Vanderdick looked down at his son and smiled. Then he said to Mrs. Periwinkle, "You know, this bet idea isn't so crazy. I don't see how we can lose. No way that runty kid beats my son. I'll have the lawyers put together a new agreement. You'll be counting your millions in no time."

"*Millions*," she repeated dreamily.

"And now," Vanderdick announced, "it's time Todd and I got out there and enjoyed Secret Special Visitors Day!"

"Wait!" Mrs. Lutzkraut exclaimed. "You haven't tried my famous egg salad sandwiches yet."

As much as I hated Todd and his father, I almost screamed, "Run!" I remembered those putrid sandwiches from all the times I had to sit in her classroom during recess.

Vanderdick excused himself with a "Next time" and headed toward the door. Then he stopped dead in his tracks and put his hand to his ear. "Wait. What's that?"

I listened, but all I heard was the sound of kids in the distance shouting and having fun.

"What is it?" Mr. Periwinkle asked.

Vanderdick faced him with a big grin. "I thought I could already hear the bulldozers knocking down your forest!" With that, he and Todd burst out laughing and walked away under the midday sun.

"Why did you come up with that bet?" I asked Mr. Periwinkle as we headed down the hill to join the other campers. He had volunteered to be my Special Visitor after the mean trick played on me by Mrs. Lutzkraut.

"Well, Rodney, that's tough to answer, but maybe you'll understand when you're a bit older. You see, Todd's father and I go back a long way, and he has always thought himself much better than me. I guess I just got sick of it back at the house and decided to challenge him. If you and the other Cherokees can win the race, it would be the greatest day in the history of Camp Wy-Mee."

"Yeah, and if we lose it will be the *last* day of Camp Wy-Mee."

We walked along in silence for a while and soon found ourselves by the old beech tree. "What he said was true, you know," Mr. Periwinkle continued. "I, too, was in the Cherokee cabin. I was your age, and they called us losers even then. Every year we would come up short, but this year we won't. This year, we have a secret weapon. This year, we have Rodney Rathbone— New York junior yachting champ! I know you never wanted to boast about it, but I overhead you earlier this summer . . . when you told that Tabitha girl at sign-up for expert sailing class."

Not knowing how to respond, I stared out at the pines and oaks and wondered what kind of desserts the new Applebee's would serve.

Chapter 20

MY LIPS ARE SEALED

The next morning after breakfast Mr. Periwinkle met my cabinmates and me down by the dock.

"Okay, boys," he began, "I suppose by now Rodney has filled you in on the canoe race and what's at stake." Everyone nodded. "Good. Now let me explain the race. Each boys' cabin has to put one canoe team into the event. That means twelve cabins will have a canoe in the race. Each year we have a winning team, but this year, even if we don't come in first, we have to finish ahead of the Algonquins."

"Who won last year?" Stinky asked.

"The Algonquins, but—"

"How about the year before that?" Thorin asked.

"The Algonquins. Now if—"

"How about the—"

"Look! They've won for the last twenty years or more. Let's not dwell on minor details, okay? Back to the race. It takes two days. You will canoe all day Saturday on the Drownalott River, camp out at Skull Rock, and finish the race on Sunday. The team that finishes first on Saturday will have a head start Sunday morning. If you finish ten minutes off the pace Saturday, you have to wait ten minutes Sunday morning. Make sense? Any questions so far?"

Josh raised his hand.

"Yes, Josh?"

"What's a canoe?"

No one answered. What could we say? I finally pointed to a canoe floating next to the dock. Josh walked over and examined it.

"That's a boat." He smiled proudly.

"A canoe *is* a boat," I explained.

Mr. Periwinkle shook his head from side to side. Eventually his gaze returned to the rest of us. "Where was I? Oh yes, the canoe always has two paddlers and a person sitting in the middle. I've given some thought to who should be on our team. Rodney, you're a no-brainer. We already know what kind of boatman you are. I assume a sailing champion can handle one of these?" My stomach tightened. Mr. Periwinkle scanned the lot of us. "Who else? Thorin, what do you know about being out on the water?"

Thorin stepped forward. "I know the Lady of the Lake rose from the waters and gave King Arthur"—he lifted both arms in the air for effect—"Excalibur!"

Mr. Periwinkle's smile lingered strangely for a

moment. "That's wonderful. Now, why don't you go stand over there?" He pointed inland, away from the dock. "Fernando, do you think you're up to the race?"

Fernando smiled and nodded. "Mr. Periwinkle, Fernando has many talents. Tell me, how many women will be at this . . . Skull Rock?"

Mr. Periwinkle gave a nervous giggle. "Maybe you could keep Thorin company." He looked at Stinky, who wasn't listening. His attention seemed occupied by whatever lay deep within his nose. Mr. Periwinkle flinched.

Josh was still staring at the canoe. Mr. Periwinkle walked over next to him and looked down. "Handling a canoe can be tough, my boy. Do you have any experience?"

Josh punched his fist into his palm. "I can handle anything tough."

"Can you paddle?"

Josh turned to him and practically yelled, "I can paddle, punch, bash, maul, crunch, punch, bash, punch, uhh, punch!"

"I think we've found our man." Mr. Periwinkle turned back to the rest of us. "This year, there's been a change of rule. You see, in order for Camp Wy-Mee to avoid a Title Nine lawsuit"—at the mention of the word *lawsuit* he gave a little shiver—"there must be a third person in the canoe. And that person must be one of the girls from camp."

Fernando left Thorin and hovered near Mr. Periwinkle with renewed attention.

Periwinkle continued, "I believe this is a distinct advantage for us. You see, I've noticed that one of you is quite gifted when it comes to courting young ladies . . ."

"Some call it a gift, some fools say it's a curse. I don't know why things are the way they are, but ever since Fernando was a little niño, I've—"

Mr. Periwinkle interrupted, "I'm sorry, Fernando, this is a busy week and the speeches will have to wait. As I was saying, young Rodney here holds the interest of a girl who knows boats and the water. You know who I'm referring to, right, Rodney?"

I knew, but after her comments at the cotillion dinner, I wasn't so sure I could count on Tabitha to join our team. I didn't say anything. Periwinkle added, "We need Tabitha and her boating skills, Rodney. With her on board, we'll have an excellent shot at winning. In fact, it's probably our best chance. Now, everyone, off to your next activity!"

The pressure was on—and it wasn't even nine thirty in the morning. This was going to be some day.

News of the race and the bet had traveled throughout the camp. Most people no longer saw us as the "losers." We, and especially yours truly, were the saviors of the forest, the defenders of the lake, and the knights of all things good. If I had wanted, I could have been carried around that week in an Adirondack chair or even a canoe. You'd think I would have enjoyed all the attention, but to be honest, there's nothing comforting about everyone depending on you when you know the truth—that you're only going to let them down.

Right after my meeting with Mr. Periwinkle, on my way to arts and crafts, was when I first noticed the attention. Countless people patted me on the back and wished me good luck. As I walked along, even the birds seemed to sing more and the insects bite less. I shrugged this off as some weird natural occurrence, but when the bushes bordering the soccer field said, "Beat those jerks, Rodney," my throat ran dry and I strongly considered a visit to the camp infirmary for a psych evaluation. Before I went, I remembered what my aunt had once told me: *Madness is no excuse for bad manners.* I answered, "Thank you, errr . . . Mr. Bush."

Survival Steve's head popped out from between the branches. "Mr. Bush? What are you going on about? Rodney, do you know that Vanderdick is planning to turn my shack into a Starbucks?"

I pictured a cappuccino machine with antlers.

"Are you listening, Rodney?"

"Sure."

"Well, I know quite a bit about canoes. Built one myself once."

"Did you make it out of moose skin and bear bones?"

"Nope, I used an advanced fiberglass polymer. I've

taken that canoe down the Snake River, the Mohawk River, the Rio Grande, and the Colorado. You bring your team down to the canoe beach tomorrow night and we'll work on your skills." His head dropped back into the bush.

After what seemed like a few hundred pats on the back and high-fives, I finally arrived at arts and crafts. I had just started the class the week before. Alison told me to sign up for it. While I loved going to art museums back in New York City with Aunt Evelyn and my parents, I wasn't the most skilled at putting together the little crafts projects Sunshine, the art counselor, had waiting for me. This didn't matter much, since Sunshine spent most of the time weaving flowers in her hair and smiling.

I sat down next to Alison, feeling stressed out. I definitely wasn't in the mood to be creative with so much riding on me. Alison looked like she wanted to talk. She was just opening her mouth when Sunshine stepped out of the shed—only it wasn't Sunshine.

"I don't believe it," I managed to utter.

"Believe it, mister," Mrs. Lutzkraut said. "I'm keeping a close eye on you and your inevitable mischief." She leaned down above me as she said it, and we held each other's gaze until the prolonged sight of her awful face made me queasy. I looked down and she announced, "Good morning, boys and girls. I'm afraid Sunshine has taken ill. My name is Mrs. Lutzkraut. I thought I'd fill in, as I have been a teacher for some years. Now, today you may make either a clay sculpture, or an architectural design out of Popsicle sticks. Rodney, after looking at last week's attempt at creating a mosaic, let me suggest you stick to clay."

Alison turned to me. "I heard all about the canoe race. I also heard you had to pick a girl to join you. So who are you picking?"

Alison, who was usually so calm and cool, looked unusually eager. I could see a problem looming. I began, "*Well* . . ."

"I just want you to understand that I know how important winning the race is, and I want you to know I'm ready."

"Um, are you a good canoer?" I asked, squeezing some clay.

"My grandpa has one in his garage."

"Have you ever been in it?"

"The garage?"

"No, the canoe!"

"Not really."

"How about another canoe?"

"No."

"A kayak?"

"No."

"A rowboat?"

"No."

"Have you ever been in a boat?"

"Of course, Rodney. My family took a Disney cruise last winter."

"You realize a cruise ship is a little bigger than a canoe, right?"

"Duh, Rodney. What's that got to do with anything?"

Why couldn't the girl I found myself liking more and more be the boating expert? I doubted asking Tabitha would help my relationship with Alison. In thinking of girl problems, I cringed as I remembered hanging up on Jessica the other night at the Periwinkles'. Nothing was going right.

"Can you swim at least?" I asked.

"Of course I can swim, Rodney. I even won a race at swimming last week."

Finally, some good news! Having a fast swimmer in the boat could be important. I felt more hopeful as I pictured her freestyling across the water. "What stroke did you use?"

"Doggy paddle."

"Uh, yeah. I missed that stroke in the last Olympics." My brief feeling of optimism left me like air rushing from a deflating balloon. "How about I talk it over with Josh and let you know later?"

She seemed to accept that. Happy to avoid continuing the conversation, I worked on my sculpture of a cobra and thought about all the mounting pressures facing me.

A little later Mrs. Lutzkraut strolled by. "Let's see what you've managed for us today, Rodney." I had rolled coils of clay together into a spiral to look like a snake getting ready to strike. "And what is that?" she asked.

"A snake."

"A snake? It looks like something my neighbor's dog

leaves on the lawn. For that revolting little creation you can clean up today's mess. Everyone else, off you go to your next activity."

The group dispersed. Alison lingered to help me but Mrs. Lutzkraut shooed her away. Under my old teacher's amused, evil eye, I scrambled to pick everything up. I jammed the Popsicle sticks and glue sticks into boxes to carry to the shed. One glue stick rolled off the table. As I bent down to get it, Mrs. Lutzkraut announced, "You know, Rodney, when we start building here we're going to make an exclusive private school for the Dry Lake Condo Community." She was sitting in a chair fanning herself. I stuck the glue stick in my pocket and turned to face her.

"What makes you think you're going to start building? This camp is staying just the way it is."

She ignored my comment and asked, "Do you think I should make myself principal of the new school? What would you think of that?"

"I've always thought you'd make an excellent warden," I answered, stuffing a pair of scissors back into their holster.

"That's right. Keep those fresh comments coming. I'm going to take enormous satisfaction the rest of my years knowing that my life's greatest victory—and most profitable moment—came with your defeat. This weekend will be such fun. I can hardly wait." She glanced at her watch. "I need to go meet with the architects. Off you go. Run along!"

She didn't need to tell me twice. Normally, I wouldn't be in a rush to get to my second activity with Cramps, but I knew Tabitha would be walking there too, and I needed to speak with her. I realized that this might mean an end with Alison, but I also knew Periwinkle was right. She was the most talented boater in camp. I scrambled along quickly, trying not to attract attention from my new fans.

I spotted her walking on the other side of the softball field in the direction of the volleyball courts, where Mr. Cramps awaited. I whistled. Her head turned and she started to make her way across the field toward me. Her long brown hair blew in the hot summer wind, and I felt a strong need to make a good impression. I pushed my hair down, smelled my breath, and felt around in my pocket for the lip balm stick my mom had packed. I pulled it out and rubbed it across my lips as Tabitha gave me a little wave.

It took a couple of minutes for us to meet in center-field. She was the first to speak. "I thought I'd be hearing from you today," she said. "Did you know that Todd was waiting for me outside my cabin this morning? He asked me to join his canoe team."

I didn't like where this was going. I was worried. Was I already too late? I also began to worry about an odd tingling sensation on my lips.

She kept talking. "I told him I'd think about it, but the truth is, I'm not sure yet. So why'd you whistle? Do you have something to ask me?" Her smile told me I had a chance.

Well, she couldn't have made that any easier, I thought to myself. I went to open my mouth to invite her on the team, but I just couldn't do it. It wasn't that I had lost my nerve. My lips were actually sealed shut! "MMMM-MMmmmmmmm!" was all I could utter.

"Mmmmmm? You're eating something tasty?" She looked confused.

"MMMMMMMM!" This time I waved my hands in the air and started jumping up and down.

Her face went from confused to angry. "How rude! I turned Todd down because I figured I would be on your team, and now you stand there acting like an ape."

"MMMmmmmMMMM." I pointed to my mouth. Then I grabbed my lips with my hands and pulled. They wouldn't budge.

Tabitha didn't wait while I struggled. She made a look of disgust and shouted, "You're a weirdo! What did I see in you? I'm joining Todd's team!"

My lips finally ripped open. The pain was immense. "Aaarrghhh!" I yelled. My eyes welled up with tears, making it difficult to see. The one thing I noticed was Tabitha moving away rapidly. That was bad enough, but I apparently had even worse things to deal with. What was wrong with me? Did I have lockjaw? I remembered the lip balm. What had my mom given me? I yanked it out of my pocket and read the label: OLD HORSE SUPER STRONG GLUE STICK.

I had grabbed it while cleaning up for Lutzkraut! There was no way she could have known—or could she? Either way, the outcome was the same. My team's odds of beating the Algonquins had now dropped from bad to impossible.

By the time dinner rolled around, I was feeling almost numb, like a prisoner resigned to his fate. The weekend's race would be a disaster, and I was on the way to my last meal. Two people waited for me by the dining hall entrance. Periwinkle spoke first. "Did you get her? Did you get Tabitha?" He looked eager, but at the mention of Tabitha's name, the other person frowned.

I looked over at Alison. Her beautiful eyes looked into mine and I suddenly felt happy. "I was lucky enough to get someone better," I explained.

"Really? Who?" Mr. Periwinkle asked.

"Mr. Periwinkle, this is Alison. She's completing the dream team."

Alison tried hard to conceal her smile, but you could tell it was just the news she was waiting for. "Thanks, captain," she whispered.

"Well, now, Alison," Mr. Periwinkle asked as he turned to enter the dining hall. "Tell me about your paddling experience."

"Actually," she answered proudly, "I just won a paddle race last week."

"Really?" Mr. Periwinkle clapped his hands together and beamed at me. "Well done, Rodney. I knew you'd come through!"

Chapter 21

A RAT ON THE SHORE

Twelve aluminum canoes lined a sandy stretch along the bank of the Drownalott River. Each team, along with the Periwinkles, Mrs. Lutzkraut, Survival Steve, Mr. Cramps, a host of other camp personnel, and a few random campers, had made the long van trek to the starting point of the big race. The day was hot, which added to the tension that hung over the gathering.

Mr. Periwinkle adjusted his pith helmet. "We're all set to start the race. You know the rules. Today you will paddle for ten miles to Skull Rock. You'll spend the night there. Along the way, Mrs. Periwinkle and I will watch you from various checkpoints, which are accessible by Jeep. Mr. Cramps will be in the Zodiac motor boat and Steve will be in his own canoe . . . in case you need assistance out on the water."

I didn't like the sound of that and wondered what kind of assistance we might need. I didn't like any of this.

A couple of months ago I had never even heard of Camp Wy-Mee. Now its fate rested on my shoulders, all because Mrs. Lutzkraut was prepared to stop at nothing to get rich. She stood behind Mr. Periwinkle, looking in my direction. I couldn't tell if she was frowning or smiling. All I knew was that she was up to something. But what?

Mr. Periwinkle continued. "At Skull Rock we will record your time and start you accordingly tomorrow morning for the final leg of the race . . . "

He went on blabbing about the rules and I found myself zoning out, like I did in school. I looked off into the woods. I wasn't the only one not paying attention. Woo appeared to be singing with several frogs. He saw me and shouted, "They're doing bebop!" As usual I didn't know what he was saying and just smiled. He turned back to the frogs and yelled, "Go, man, go!"

"Rodney, please pay attention," Mr. Periwinkle scolded. "As you might imagine, this is all very important. Now, tonight we will have a cookout, and then we'll split into two groups. The boys will be sleeping in an area with me, Mr. Cramps, and Steve, and Mrs. Lutzkraut and Mrs. Periwinkle will be camping with the girls. Your sleeping gear and tents have already been delivered to the site. The food will be dropped off later."

Under other circumstances, the race actually sounded like a great time. Too bad there was so much riding on it.

"Okay, does anyone have any questions?"

Antsy to get started, I prayed no one did. Unfortunately,

Skip raised his hand. He was standing next to his big jerk canoe partner, Todd. "Mr. Periwinkle?" he began.

"Yes, Skip?"

"I, um, I . . ." Suddenly he grabbed his stomach and fell to the floor.

"Oh no, what's the matter?" Mrs. Lutzkraut yelled, rushing over to the Algonquin canoe. "What is it, son?"

Son? I had never heard her speak nicely to anyone. Something was up. Skip rolled around on the ground holding his stomach. Todd leaned over him. "It's his stomach, Mr. Periwinkle. There is no way he can race. We'll need a substitute canoer."

"How dreadful," Mrs. Lutzkraut said, but a look on her face—combined with some pretty poor acting by Skip and Todd—told me this was all fake. "Todd," she asked, "do you have anyone in mind to replace Skip?"

"Well, now that you mention it, what about . . . hmmm . . . Magnus?"

Mr. Periwinkle jumped in. "Hold on a minute, this is a camper race. Magnus is a counselor. He's twice your size. He's not allowed to participate."

"Percy," Mrs. Lutzkraut observed, "I see you haven't consulted the rules. They clearly state counselors are allowed to race."

"Helga, the rules don't say that. They—"

Mrs. Lutzkraut yanked a book from her purse and thrust it at Mr. Periwinkle. "It says so right here on page forty-three."

Mr. Periwinkle looked. "This is nothing. The rules have been crossed out and someone wrote new ones in pencil. They've been changed . . ."

"Changed by me, as camp director!" she snapped. "I am majority owner, and I feel it's much safer to have some counselors out on the water. If you're worried about fairness, you may certainly replace Joshua or Rodney with Woo."

Everyone turned to look at Woo. He was still hunched over the frogs, singing. Mr. Periwinkle bit his lip.

Magnus spoke up next. "Goot ting I just happen to have my paddle." He pulled out a cello case from the back of a van. Was he going to join Woo in a duet? He set the case on the ground and I leaned forward to watch. He clicked open the clasps and lifted the lid. A shiny, dark, wooden paddle lay surrounded by purple velvet. "Dis beauty helped me win the Scandinavian Rafting Championship on the Sjoa River three years in a row."

Mrs. Lutzkraut acted surprised. "A rafting champion? Who would have guessed? My, Percy, you've really recruited a talented staff this year."

Mr. Periwinkle didn't respond. Instead, he gathered Alison, Josh, and me to the side. His face looked very tense, and I understood why. Todd and Tabitha were already heavy favorites. Adding a Scandinavian rafting champ made them unbeatable.

He swallowed hard and cleared his throat. I could tell a big speech was coming. "Okay, this is it," he began.

"It's time. Remember, they're bigger than you. They're faster and more experienced. They've canoed longer and they fight dirtier . . ."

If he's trying to build our confidence, he's going about it in a weird way, I thought.

". . . Not one Cherokee team has ever won, and the Algonquins almost never lose. Right now, Vegas has you listed as a thousand-to-one underdog . . ."

Now that Magnus was in their canoe, that didn't seem high enough.

". . . Furthermore, if you don't win, everything will be destroyed. All these trees you see in every direction will be cut down. All the animals will die. The world will be one step closer to global warming and ruin. Simply put, this is the most important canoe race in the history of mankind." His eyes looked wet and his skin was changing color, but then he exhaled and seemed to gather himself a little. "Anyway, the important thing is to have fun!" He gave us each a pat on the back and walked off into the woods, where he hugged a tree and collapsed.

"Well, that certainly made me feel a lot better," I said to Alison.

"Yeah, real inspiring."

"Okay, racers, into your boats!" Mrs. Lutzkraut called. She was holding a cap gun and was ready to start the race.

If canoes had names, ours should have been the

S.S. Impossible! Josh, Alison, and I climbed in. We were about to embark on the most important canoe race in the history of mankind . . . or something like that.

Satisfied that she had everyone's attention, Mrs. Lutzkraut shouted, "Get on your mark. Get set. Go!" She fired her cap gun. Maybe it was just my imagination, but I think it was pointed right at me.

We pushed the canoe out into the water. The sand made a grating noise as it scraped the bottom of the aluminum. We banged into other canoes and paddles as we jostled to get out into the river.

Josh sat in the front, swinging his paddle wildly. I couldn't be sure if he was trying to whack a turtle or clobber Todd, but either way Tabitha was getting splashed and screaming at him from the Algonquin boat. This had Alison laughing, and I would have joined her but Mr. Periwinkle's encouraging words, "Everything will die," echoed in my ears. I yelled, "Josh, start paddling!"

He looked back at me with a vague expression.

"Remember what Steve showed you?" As I said this I mimicked the basic pull with my paddle and Josh slowly began to nod. I nodded, too, as encouragement. Josh's paddle dipped into the water and off we went.

Once he got the hang of it, it didn't take long for us to find a rhythm. Alison sat in the middle of the canoe on the floor. The middle person doesn't paddle but can usually switch when one of the two paddlers gets tired. The rear of the canoe, where I sat, is reserved for the person who does the steering. And while I may never become a sailor, I took to canoeing fairly quickly. True to his promise, Survival Steve had spent the past few days working with us on a variety of paddle strokes and techniques. Josh, on the other hand, learned only one. He could paddle the basic front pull stroke—but that was enough. His tremendous strength made this one basic paddle stroke long and swift.

I felt him pull us along. I dug deep in the water, also pulling hard, and I kept us going straight down the middle of the river.

It wasn't long before ten canoes fell back behind us, which was encouraging but not good enough. It was the eleventh canoe that mattered. I glanced over at it. Todd was in the front, pulling long, even strokes. While he wasn't able to rival Josh's power, it was obvious he knew what he was doing. And then there was Magnus. It was easy to believe he had won those championships. Being a big, full-grown counselor, he had every bit of Josh's strength. As I watched his fancy paddle caress the surface of the water, I realized that he also possessed all of Steve's expertise. Tabitha sat in the middle and occasionally gave me a nasty look.

For over an hour we battled hard, grunting from the strain. I couldn't help notice that Todd and Magnus seemed to be struggling, too. Catching my eye, Todd yelled, "Give it up, Rathbone!" I ignored him but he continued. "Guess what? With the profits from the construction, my dad's getting me a Ferrari."

Tabitha almost fell out of the canoe. "Really, Toddy? Your own Ferrari? Will it be red?"

"Sure," he answered, smirking back at me. I wished I had some snappy reply but my mouth was dry from breathing hard, and as much as it disgusted me, I knew Tabitha would look good in the front seat of a Ferrari. Besides, what could I offer her? A ride in my father's old Honda?

We were beginning to fall back. My shoulders and back burned and I fought off annoying thoughts of Todd and Tabitha zooming by in a red sports car. I eyed the back of Alison's head. Why couldn't she be some big Scandinavian canoe girl who could give me a few minutes rest? All Alison ever managed to do when we practiced was drop the paddle overboard and scream. Really, other than making the canoe heavier, she wasn't doing anything. She was, as Survival Steve had put it, dead weight.

Then she turned back to me. Her red hair spun out over the water as she turned. I could see her brown eyes through her sunglasses, and I thought, *That's the prettiest dead weight I've ever seen. . . .* She smiled and said, "Keep going, you're doing great. Did I ever tell you that you look cute canoeing?"

"Thanks," Josh grunted.

Alison and I both laughed. I shrugged off my previous feelings. I felt happy she was with us, and the Ferrari thoughts didn't bother me much after that.

What bothered me was the fact that, try as we might, we couldn't keep pace with Todd and Magnus.

And then we came around a bend and caught our first break.

Several yellow ropes were tied across the river. A big red sign stated: DANGER. WATERFALL. PORTAGE TO RIGHT. A portage meant we had to paddle to the side and carry our canoe on land for a while. If you ignored the sign and somehow pushed under the ropes, a twenty-foot drop and probable death awaited you. I figured if we couldn't beat them on the water, maybe we could pass them on land.

Todd reached the bank first. We were about ten yards behind. The three of us jumped out, pulled the canoe high up on the bank, rolled it over, and hoisted it over our heads.

They say aluminum is a wonder metal because it is strong and light. It wasn't long, however, before the wonderful lightness faded and my arms and shoulders began to burn from the strain of constant lifting without a break. Alison, to her credit, held up the middle of the canoe and grunted right along with us. To carry a canoe any distance, you have to put it over your head and hold it shoulder-height as you walk along. Our heads would occasionally crack against the inside of the canoe. Having your head stuck within a canoe makes vision difficult, and right away we were stumbling and going off course.

But that wasn't the worst part. Unfortunately, half the

mosquitoes in Ohio suddenly decided to pay us a visit.

They announced their assault with their famous, high-pitched, "Eeeeeeeeeeee" noise. One of them circled my head and bounced off my forehead and neck. Then it landed on the tip of my nose. It sat there for a second, looking me in the eye. I went cross-eyed returning the stare. I'm sure it was my imagination, but it seemed to be smiling, and then . . . *chomp*. I felt the little sting, and even worse, I saw all of the little vampire's friends zooming in under the canoe's metal edge to join the fun.

The attack was on—and it was a one-sided battle. If I used my hand to whack them, I'd drop the canoe on my skull. It wasn't long before all three of us were cursing and whining. The mosquitoes, realizing their victims were helpless, charged with greater ferocity. I tried shaking my head, or blowing hard puffs of air at them, but nothing worked. I was close to going insane.

In the end, it was Alison who saved us. "Boys, I'm going to let go. The load will get heavier but I'll squash the mosquitoes!" She let go and started slapping us.

"Slap harder!" I yelled. "Get the one on my neck!"

"And my legs," Josh called out.

After about two minutes of Alison waving her arms and slapping us silly, the bites slowed and my sanity returned.

Not everyone, however, had found relief. From up ahead we heard Magnus shout, "Deese bugs drive me crazy!" followed by a large BOOM. We paused and lifted the canoe higher to see. The Algonquin canoe had fallen, rolled down a hill, and gotten wedged between two boulders. Magnus was jumping around and scratching at his face.

"The canoe!" Todd shouted. "We have to get it!"

"Deese bugs! No bugs like deese in da fjords!" Magnus tore off toward the river.

With Alison managing our bug problem, this was our chance to pull ahead. We hurried past our Algonquin enemies and I caught a glimpse of Magnus plunging his head underwater. Tabitha was whining about a broken fingernail and Todd was busy trying to remove a mud stain from his shirt. They definitely appeared to be a defeated team.

We reached the riverbank below the waterfall and resumed the race. Once underway, I looked back. Their canoe was stuck in an awkward spot and Tabitha and Todd were struggling to get Magnus out of the river.

The lead was now ours. Alison turned to me from her spot in the middle and yelled, "It would take a miracle for them to catch up to us today!" You could see she was happy and proud. I smiled back, but it was only for her benefit. She had never spent an entire school year in Mrs. Lutzkraut's class. I knew it was only a matter of time before our luck changed.

We were still paddling hard, but slower and more consistently. It had been an hour since we left the Alqonguins.

The Drownalott River had lots of twists and turns. There was no way of knowing how far ahead we were or how much time the Algonquins had lost trying to free their canoe. Alison, who was proving her worth again and again, spotted Mr. and Mrs. Periwinkle on the side of the river.

Mr. Periwinkle was running and jumping along the bank. "You have the lead! Way to go! Only two miles left to Skull Rock. Wa-hoo!" Josh and Alison waved at him and cheered back.

I didn't join them. I was watching the opposite bank. Mrs. Lutzkraut had emerged from behind a boulder. She had her hands on a walkie-talkie and I could see her mouth moving a mile a minute. I noticed a large bag of some kind by her side. She caught my gaze. I had hoped to see panic in her eyes, but they held an evil confidence that shook me.

"Paddle faster!" I hollered.

The canoe wobbled as Josh's thrusts increased. I knew something was about to happen. I could just feel it. I looked around. The river was calm. Bugs danced on the surface of the water. Maybe I was wrong. Maybe nothing bad was coming.

And then I heard it.

Vrrooooom! It was a motor and it was gaining on us. I looked back at a bend in the river just in time to see a rubber motorboat zooming our way. Cramps! I knew he'd be making an appearance. His comb-over flapped in the wind like a weird pirate flag as he bore down on us. Would he actually ram us? I didn't think he would go that far, but I also knew who we were up against. Lutzkraut and her henchmen were determined to win at any cost.

Josh turned back and smiled. "Cool!"

"No, Josh," I shouted. "Definitely not cool."

Cramps was about to smash us but veered to the right at the last second, sending a huge wake over the bow of the canoe and knocking Josh back onto Alison. The canoe rocked violently. I had to lean in and balance to keep it from going over.

"Did I get you kids wet?" Cramps yelled with an evil smile. "Gee, that's too bad. Don't tell your mommies." He gave a little laugh and zoomed away up the river.

Alison was sitting in six inches of water. "Forget about him," she suggested. "Let's keep going. You two paddle and I'll bail out the water."

We resumed paddling, but with the added water the boat was heavier and harder to move. Fortunately, like some big plow horse, Josh didn't seem to notice and never tired. He kept pulling us along.

Was that the best Lutzkraut could do? I wondered. It would take more than a little wave to stop me from saving Camp Wy-Mee. I could feel confidence filling my chest. I was beginning to wonder whether Todd, Magnus, and Tabitha had even gotten their canoe free from the boulders.

"Look!" Alison screamed. She was pointing in back of me. My confidence turned to indigestion as I whirled around, half expecting to see Lutzkraut bearing down on us in a gunboat.

The reality was almost as bad. Coming around the bend was Todd's pink shirt and perfect hair. Seeing me look back, he and Tabitha gave little waves.

Alison bailed faster, and Josh and I dug in for more frantic pulling. Already I could feel blisters forming on my hands. My back and shoulders and arms and, well, everywhere ached. We still led by more than a hundred yards, but despite all our effort, the lead had dwindled. I couldn't believe how fast they were gaining—and yet they hardly seemed to be paddling.

"There's Skull Rock!" Alison yelled, pointing ahead. She was right, and I immediately saw why they called it that. An ancient rock the size of a house stuck out from a cliff above the river. It looked just like a human skull. Below it, tents dotted the shore. My stomach did a nervous flip as I realized that this is where we would be spending the night.

"Eat our wake, losers!" Todd yelled. I jumped and nearly tipped the canoe. How could they be right next to us already? Magnus and Tabitha weren't even paddling! They were busy lifting something into a duffel bag.

"What's in the bag?" I called over to Tabitha, trying to regain my calm. I wanted to act like I was unconcerned that they had overtaken us.

"Suddenly you remember how to talk?" she sneered, zipping the bag shut. It was then that I realized I had seen the bag before. I was sure it was the one I had seen Mrs. Lutzkraut carrying earlier.

I was about to ask, when Magnus gripped his paddle and swung it over his head like a deranged Viking. "Yaaa!" he roared, smashing it onto the water's surface. A great splash shot our way and hit me in my open mouth. I spit out the river water.

As they pulled away, Todd yelled back, "Hey, Rathbone, you really did eat our wake. What a loser!"

I could only gape, dumbfounded. The three of them didn't even look tired. For a few seconds, Josh, Alison, and I stared blankly. This was nothing new for Josh, of course, but Alison and I were coming to the same conclusion. We had somehow lost the day's competition.

"Come on, let's get to camp," she said sadly.

Exhausted, we continued the rest of the way in silence, finally paddling up to Skull Rock a full four minutes behind the Algonquin canoe. With our big lead lost, it was doubtful we could catch them tomorrow. In fact, it was looking doubtful that anyone but construction workers would be visiting Camp Wy-Mee next summer.

Chapter 22

SKULL ROCK

I climbed from the canoe with Skull Rock staring down at me through the darkening sky. Just seconds before, out on the water, I had been upset about losing the lead to Todd and Magnus. Now, as I looked around at the clearing of dirt between the river and the creepy woods, a different fear gripped me. I would be spending the night in a tent in the middle of nowhere surrounded by some of my worst enemies. If the bears didn't get me, Todd would.

"Hey, Josh, great paddling back there," I said, making sure to stay close by his side.

"Uhhh, thanks," he answered. "Look." He was gazing proudly at a beetle he had just squished on a rock.

Alison shook her head. "Gross. Come on, guys, let's join the others."

The three of us wandered toward the clearing. I was happy to see Survival Steve's white van parked back in the bushes next to an overgrown dirt road. Mr. Periwinkle met me. "What happened out there? You had the lead."

I shrugged. My mind still couldn't make sense of how the other canoe passed us so quickly.

Periwinkle looked glum. All he said was, "Your gear is leaning against the van. Set up your tent and start gathering firewood. You don't want to be out here in the dark without a tent or a fire." His tone suggested that he really meant it, and I didn't wait around to be told again.

For the next hour I sat on the ground, trying to figure out the tent instructions. After finally assembling what looked like a sagging hot air balloon with poles sticking out, I headed into the woods to gather twigs and branches. I made sure not to go too far. The last thing I needed was to get lost again, like on the way up to Camp Wy-Mee.

I made several trips, and each time I returned to camp I noticed that another canoe team had arrived. It felt better with more people there, but it was still pretty scary, and getting dark real fast. The large stones and boulders at the bottom of Skull Rock formed a sinister smile that seemed to grin right at me. This was going to be a long night.

I decided to head back into the forest for one final haul of firewood. This time, I had to walk further in to find any. It was almost night now and I began to feel that maybe I had wandered off too far. When a wild animal started shrieking across the river, I spun around to head back to Josh and Alison. I hadn't gotten very far when

I bumped into two people, but not the two I wanted.

"Woot have we here?" Magnus asked.

"Is that you, Rathbone?" Todd demanded, peering at me through the dark. "You shouldn't be out this far all alone. Legend has it Skull Rock is cursed." I wasn't going to argue with him on that one. I tried to walk past but he stopped me with a shove to the shoulder. "What's the rush?" He leaned in closer. This wasn't good. Todd was pumped up, toughness no doubt coming easier with Magnus standing behind him. "Upset you're going to lose the race?"

"Like he ever hood a chance," Magnus gloated.

Todd laughed. "Come out here to cry, Rathbone?"

They couldn't see my face in the dark, and it was a good thing, too. I actually *did* feel a little teary. I was wishing I was back home in my bed instead of standing in these scary woods with two idiots. My home, and even Camp Wy-Mee, seemed like a world away.

Fortunately, my focus shifted from fright-inspired homesickness to the matter at hand. Knowing something awful was about to happen, and knowing my shaking chicken knees were going to give me away, I came up with a brilliant escape plan.

"Your shoes are untied." I pointed to their feet. I knew such an old and obvious trick didn't stand a chance, but I was desperate.

CLUNK!

I was so shocked to see their two heads bang together

that I almost didn't run. As the echo began to fade, my feet kicked into gear and I slipped through several bushes and dodged in and out of the trees.

Magnus boomed after me, "Nice try, but you can't trick ooos."

Under other circumstances I might have stopped and pointed out that I *had* just tricked them, but I kept moving.

"We'll get you later, Rathbone!" Todd yelled. "Better not leave the fire and your buddy Josh."

I ran straight through the woods until I emerged in the clearing. Steve was crouching over the fire ring, a few small flames dancing on the kindling. Everyone was crowded around him. No doubt the creepy surroundings were affecting them, too. I joined Mr. Periwinkle, Alison, and Josh.

"Look at you, Rodney," Alison said. "You look like you've just seen a ghost."

"He probably did," Steve replied, cracking a branch over his knee. "Plenty of ghosts out here by Skull Rock. There was a massacre here during the French and Indian War."

Mr. Periwinkle shivered more than me. "Remind me," he asked Steve, "why we have to camp here every year?"

Steve smiled. "What could be better than skulls and ghosts? Now *that's* camping. Besides, it's accessible by dirt road, has a nice clearing to set up tents and build a fire, is halfway between the starting point and camp, has a gentle, sloping bank for the canoes ..."

"Okay, we get it," Mr. Periwinkle muttered impatiently. "Just hurry with that fire."

"I reckon it's going now. Anyway, Perce, when's dinner?"

"I'm not sure. Helga was taking care of the food."

For the first time I noticed Mrs. Lutzkraut. She was standing beneath a dead pine tree. Seeing her face hovering in the dim light was worse than staring at Skull Rock. From her spot, she snipped, "I'll have all of you know that Mr. Vanderdick personally offered to bring in the best steaks money can buy."

Mr. Periwinkle rubbed his hands together. "I can't wait."

"Well, keep waiting," Lutzkraut ordered her brother-in-law. "You and most of this mob are getting franks 'n' beans. The steaks are for today's first-place finishers."

I watched Magnus and Todd emerge from the woods and high-five each other. "Awesome." Todd beamed. Then he walked right over to me and whispered, "We'll get you later."

I pretended I didn't hear him and tried to keep my mind on the food situation. To be honest, I didn't share Periwinkle's disappointment. At that point, after a hard day on the water, I was real hungry and franks 'n' beans didn't sound bad at all. Spending the night in a tent with Josh after he ate several bowls of beans—well, that would be another matter.

★ ★ ★

Half an hour later the fire had grown large and strong and I was glad I had gathered so much wood. My fellow campers and I had to slide back from the heat. It was a good campfire, but everyone was beginning to grumble. Vanderdick hadn't shown up yet.

Thirty minutes became forty. Then an hour passed, and I could hear stomachs growling in tune with the loud August bugs. *He's not coming*, I thought. *We're out here in the middle of nowhere.* Somehow, hunger made the whole place more dismal and frightening. I looked off into the trees. What was lurking in there? I peered into the blackness where the river should be. Was someone or something out there watching us? Ready to attack us as soon as the fire died down? I kept telling myself that as long as Steve was around, we'd be fine.

"I'm starving!" Tabitha moaned.

Mr. Periwinkle turned back to Mrs. Lutzkraut. "Well, where is he? He should have been here ages ago."

Taken by surprise, Mrs. Lutzkraut appeared to shove into her mouth something that looked a lot like a chocolate bar.

"Are you eating?" Mr. Periwinkle asked.

"Mmm, no, mm, I just had a tickle in my throat. It's the night air." She wiped her mouth on her sleeve. "I tried calling, but there's no cell service. I'm sure he'll be here soon."

"I doubt it," Steve said. "Only a crazy person would

try driving that road at night. Looks like dinner's on me."

He walked over to the van, reached in the back, and pulled out what looked like a bow and arrow. Josh's eyes almost popped out of his head. "Can I come with you?"

Steve seemed to think it over for a moment before answering, "Sure. Just keep real quiet."

The two of them were heading toward the woods below Skull Rock when Mr. Periwinkle whimpered, "Steeeve. We can make it one night without food. You two better not go out there." Clearly he shared my feelings about Steve—and even Josh—sticking around.

Steve laughed. "No worries, Perce. These here woods are a virtual supermarket. We'll have dinner in a jiff." And in a jiff, they disappeared into the dark.

Once they were gone the woods seemed to close in on us. The night noises grew louder and we huddled closer together. I had to pee, but there was no way I was leaving the fire. Not yet, at least.

The various small conversations that were already thin and forced died. Even Tabitha stopped complaining to Todd about his father. For the past hour she had been making nasty little comments, like, "Your dad's probably still at the country club," or "Don't those fancy cars he drives have navigation devices?" Evidently, you didn't want to be around Tabitha when she was hungry.

While we humans had fallen silent, the night was far from quiet. There were the usual insect sounds, but there were also strange and chilling hooting noises.

From across the river I could still hear that animal screeching, like it was being murdered. Sometimes I thought I heard voices, and laughter, and crying . . . all shifting around in the dark. I was so hungry and tired from canoeing that I was beginning to hallucinate. I closed my eyes and imagined I heard a roaring sound like a waterfall. It was quiet at first, but it grew and grew, till soon its roar was drowning out all other sounds.

I opened my eyes and was shocked to see that every face around the fire was on the verge of panic. Something terrible really *was* out there. It sounded like a hundred motors approaching. Was it a pack of maniacs with chainsaws?

Lights burst down from the skull's eye sockets. Everyone screamed. Several campers ran off. I was frozen in fear.

The lights grew brighter and I could tell they were reflections from the road. At once I knew what was coming. Bikers! Steve had said only crazy people would drive out here at night. What kind of crazies were coming on motorcycles?

Out of a dark dust cloud the motorcycles rumbled past the van and into the clearing. I counted six grizzly-looking guys on Harleys. As I got a better look at their horned helmets and bushy beards, any glimmer of hope that they were trucking in Vanderdick's dinner for a bunch of scared and hungry campers vanished.

They rode around in a circle, herding us closer to

the fire. The revving engines roared like savage demons, and I could barely hear the people screaming around me. One thought eclipsed all others in my mind: *I should have peed when I had a chance.*

To her credit, the only person trying to combat the bikers was Mrs. Lutzkraut. She swatted at them with her purse and howled, "Scat, you ruffians!"

After several minutes of chaos and terror, they parked their bikes and turned off the engines. The cloud settled and they walked toward us. One of them stepped out before the others. He was big and frightening, with a bushy orange mustache that hung down way below his chin. He frowned, rolled his head from side to side, and shouted, "What d'you think you're doing? You're on our family's land! I'm givin' you two minutes to pack your crap and get out of here!" The other five bikers approached us with nasty smiles and dark, red eyes.

"We'll do no such thing!" Mrs. Lutzkraut yelled. "You boys are in big trouble! I'll have each of you arrested! Isn't that right, Percy?"

A bush by the edge of the woods answered, "Let's not be rash, Helga."

Ignoring the bush, one of the bikers approached Mrs. Lutzkraut. "I like my women old and feisty!" He had bad teeth and an enormous belly. He gave her a wink.

Mrs. Lutzkraut snapped, "How *dare* you? In the

public schools I've dealt with much worse than you, and I will not have—"

The leader with the long orange mustache snapped his finger in front of her face. "You ain't never dealt with the Ratfields, lady. Your chatter is givin' me a headache. One more word out of you and I'm going to toss you in the river."

While the thought of her flying into the river was oddly appealing, I was concentrating on something the biker had said. I got closer to get a better view of his face.

By now the other bikers were cracking open beer cans and yelling and laughing and scaring everyone. One of them was acting like a dog and barking at the crowd. All the while I angled over toward the leader, who stood watching his friends with his hands on his hips and a smile curled over his teeth. Suddenly one of the bikers grabbed a burning stick from the fire and started waving it around at the terrified campers.

"Todd, can't you do something?" Tabitha whispered.

Todd, who was crouching behind a shaking Magnus, had his eyes shut tight and didn't even answer.

I stepped forward and in my loudest voice declared, "*I'll* take care of this."

"Oh, thank goodness!" blurted the bush.

"Rodney, what could you possibly do?" Alison asked.

"Be careful," Tabitha added.

I didn't answer. I swung around, came up beside the

leader, and bumped his elbow. He looked down at me. I watched his smile turn to a sneer. If my plan worked, I wouldn't have to worry about Todd and Magnus or anything else. If it failed, I was about to take my last breath on this planet.

Before the biker could say anything, I stuck my right thumb up my nose and wiggled the rest of my fingers while waving my elbow up and down.

"He's gone nuts!" Mrs. Lutzkraut exclaimed.

The biker leader squinted his eyes and stared down at me. "What the . . . ? How do you know . . . ?"

"Don't you remember?" I whispered. "T-Bone, you taught it to me."

His eyes focused and they seemed to soften as he recognized me. "Ratbone? Holy smokes. I gotta tell the boys that the kid who took out the McThuggs is right here."

Even though I doubted the other campers could hear us over the crackling fire, I whispered, "Wait, T-Bone. I need a favor first. Can you just go along with whatever I say?"

He looked a bit suspicious and glanced at Lutzkraut. "You ain't gonna make me kiss the old witch, are you?"

"No, nothing that bad. Just make it like you're scared of me when I start yelling."

"Okay."

I took a step away from him and shouted, "*What* did you say? What did you call me? Do you know who you're dealing with?"

"Uh, sorry, kid. I didn't mean any disrespect."

I couldn't tell who was more shocked—the biker gang or my fellow campers.

"Sorry won't cut it!" I continued while crunching my puny knuckles. "You're coming with me. And tell your little friends to stay put and behave!"

"You're pushing it," he whispered. Then, turning to his gang, he yelled, "Hang back. Give us five."

We walked off about twenty feet into the dark and came out in a spot next to the river. "Thanks, T-Bone. Guess I got a bit carried away."

He laughed. "Ratbone, we take care of our own. By the way, what you did to the McThuggs was the talk of this year's Sturgis Motorcycle Rally—and I haven't heard a peep from J.D. and his boys in almost a year."

Back in Garrettsville, where I live, I had kind of accidentally attacked a rival biker family with a bee-hive. It's a long story, but T-Bone had tracked me down once to thank me and made me an honorary member of his family, the Ratfields. That's when he showed me the secret handshake where you stick your thumb up your nose.

"So what you wanna talk about?"

"Well, I'm in this canoe race . . ."

"That sounds cool."

"It isn't." I explained all about the race and Lutz-kraut and Vanderdick's plans for the property.

He listened and when I finished he asked, "They're going to cut down all my woods?"

I nodded.

"And build a Starbucks?"

"Yes."

"Those *are* bad people."

I nodded again.

"Well, you better win that race."

"We're already losing by over four minutes." I told him how Todd and Magnus had passed us on the river.

"They went right by you?"

"Yeah."

"What did they have in the boat with them?"

"Nothing. Just this girl Tabitha and a red duffel bag."

"What's in the bag?"

"I don't know, but I wanted to talk to you, because maybe if you ruined the race, then they wouldn't win."

He looked at me. "How would we do that? No, we can't ruin the race. If we did anything that crazy lady down there really would have us arrested." I must have looked disappointed. "But maybe I *could* help you win it."

"Really? How?" I asked.

"My family's been in these parts for years. Most people don't know about the Moonshine Canal. My great-grandpappy Rat Ratfield dug it out with his boys back in the twenties. It's a shortcut. You see, downriver, the Drownalott winds all over the place for a spell.

Moonshine Canal cuts straight through the backwoods and joins up with the river after a mile. You'll save lots of time . . . although no one really goes back in there anymore. Trust me, you don't want to meet up with any of the locals."

"Huh?"

"Never mind that. I'll tell you how to get in there. It's hidden." We talked for another couple of minutes and he told me how to find it. Then he said, "Best be getting back to the others. So, we good?"

"Uh, yeah, but could you do me one final favor?"

A minute later the kids and counselors around the fire saw the head of the biker gang come charging up from the river. "Boys, get on your bikes and ride!" he shouted frantically. "Rodney Rathbone is madder than a drunk mule and coming this way!"

They looked at him slightly confused.

"Move it or lose it!" He jumped on his motorcycle. The other bikers—seeing the biggest and baddest Ratfield take off like that—must have figured something awful was approaching, for they soon dropped what they were doing, jumped on their bikes, and rumbled off.

I ran out of the bushes with fists clenched yelling, "Where are they?"

Periwinkle emerged from his hiding spot. "You scared them off? I mean, you scared them off! Good old Rodney."

I ignored him. Instead I yelled, "I'm fired up! If I can't get my hands on those bikers, where's Todd and Magnus?" I spotted them. Making my eyes go crazy, I walked toward them. "Ready to continue our conversation?" They shook their heads and slid behind Mrs. Lutzkraut.

It took a few minutes for everyone to calm down. The group around the campfire was happy I had chased off the Ratfields, but they were confused and wanted to know what happened in the woods. I just shrugged and let their imaginations go to work.

After a while Todd said, "Too bad they ran away. I was about to show them . . ."

"Oh shut up, you wimp," Tabitha scolded. "Rodney is the only brave one around here."

"Yeah," Alison added, suddenly touching my arm. "And that's why we're going to win the canoe race tomorrow."

Just then Survival Steve, followed by Josh, burst into the firelight. "I got two possums and some wild mushrooms," he said proudly. "I'll have it all roasting in minutes. Who wants the tail? Nothing beats fresh possum tail. Did I miss anything while we were gone?"

Everyone was too shocked, and disgusted, to answer. We just stood there watching the hair crackle off the skin of the possum as Steve fussed with the fire. We were even more shocked when he cut the ratlike tail off the thing and sucked it into his mouth like a strand of spaghetti. My appetite instantly disappeared. Steve motioned to the one remaining piece of firewood. "Hey, Josh, throw that on the fire for me, will you?"

"Sure," Josh answered, not looking up from the possum he was busy examining. He walked toward the wood but came back with the red duffel bag. Before anyone could stop him, he tossed it with a thud right into the middle of the flames.

Todd, Magnus, and Lutzkraut all yelled, "Hey!"

Todd screamed at Josh, "What did you do?"

"Uh, Steve told me to throw it on the fire."

"What's that?" Mr. Periwinkle interrupted. The nylon bag had burned off and we all saw a small outboard motor lying amid the red-hot embers. Engine oil spluttered out from the metal and shot bright yellow flames into the air. Mr. Periwinkle turned towards Todd. "Why do you have an engine?"

"What? That's not mine."

"Yes, it is," I said. The mystery of their great speed on the river had been solved.

"It wasn't theirs," Mrs. Lutzkraut said. "I brought it in the van, just in case." While I knew she was lying, the evidence had burned up in front of me. In any event, Josh had taken care of one problem—and I hoped T-Bone's plan would take care of the rest.

Mr. Periwinkle stood up. "All right, everyone. We've had enough excitement for one night, and we have another big day ahead of us tomorrow. I'm sure we'll be able to get some breakfast brought out in the morning. Right now, though, time for bed."

Mr. Periwinkle was right. It had been some exciting night, but before I got into the tent there was one unfinished piece of business that needed attention. I walked to the far side of camp—away from the glow of the fire and out into the dark. I was no longer afraid of the night. In a weird way, I felt like I had conquered it. I walked a bit further down a dead-end path that came to a stop directly below Skull Rock.

As I finally took that long-overdue pee, the skull seemed to be smiling right along with me. "Good try," I said, looking up at its hollow eyes, "but it takes more than a few shrieking owls and some bikers to scare off Rodney Rathbone."

I thought I heard something move by my foot and bolted back to the tent.

Chapter 23

A FIGHT TO THE FINISH

Maybe it was just the way the sun hit it. In the morning light, Skull Rock barely looked like a skull. In fact, there was nothing scary about it at all, and the surrounding woods actually looked green and inviting. As I took down the tent, I noticed some dragonflies circling over the river. You could still smell last night's fire in the cool morning air, and I even managed a brief smile thinking about T-Bone and how everyone had thanked me afterward for running the bikers out of camp.

Yes, it should have been a great morning—the best ever—but it wasn't. It was, after all, the day that would decide the fate of Camp Wy-Mee. If we won the race, it was a day that all future generations of campers would look back on like the Fourth of July. They'd probably sing songs about me . . . maybe even put up a statue! But if we lost, well, I'd be letting down my new friends, Mr.

Periwinkle, and every tree, animal, and fish for about ten miles around.

Nothing like a little pressure to start the day.

"Okay, down to the river, everyone," Mr. Periwinkle called out. "Take your spots."

Despite Josh having tossed the Algonquin's motor in the fire, they were still beginning the race four minutes ahead of us. Sitting there and watching them paddle off was painful. Each second that clicked away on Periwinkle's stopwatch was like a teensy dagger to my gut.

I shifted anxiously on my canoe bench, waiting for our turn and looking at Alison. Earlier that morning, I had quietly explained the Moonshine Canal plan to her. Now, as I watched Todd and his crew disappear around a bend in the river, I wondered if the new plan would be enough.

"Three seconds!" Mr. Periwinkle called, looking at us briefly. "Now!"

This was it. We pushed our canoe off from the shore, jumped in, and . . .

"We're sinking!" Alison screamed. On the bank, I hadn't noticed anything strange. But she was right. The canoe instantly filled with water. "There are little holes everywhere!" she yelled as cold water came up to our necks. "Someone drilled holes in the bottom."

We had to scramble out and wade to shore, where Mrs. Lutzkraut greeted us with, "My, that was scary. It looks like your canoe is damaged and you're out of the race." Then she clutched at her heart and added, "But you're safe and that's what counts."

Survival Steve strode up carrying his canoe. "Like heck they're out of the race! Climb aboard, kids!"

"Not so fast, mister!" Mrs. Lutzkraut blocked our way. "This canoe isn't the same as the others. I'm afraid it's not regulation."

Mr. Periwinkle, who seemed unusually calm, remarked, "Well, that may have been true in the past, Helga, but I believe things have changed. After I bumped into you last night *by the water*, I took a closer look at the rules and had a talk with Steve here." He pulled Mrs. Lutztkraut's rulebook out from his back pocket. "I've particularly studied the rule rewrites you've made."

Hearing this, Mrs. Lutzkraut opened her purse and fished around for the book. Not finding it, she snarled and attempted to snatch it from Periwinkle, who flinched and ducked behind Steve. Her face began the familiar twitch that I had always assumed was caused only by me. In addition to the twitch, she bit down savagely on her lip and clenched her fingers into fists.

Mr. Periwinkle continued. "Good. Now that you seem nice and calm, I just want to point out a few interesting little tidbits. You've stated on page forty-nine that campers may use personal equipment, and that they may alter or change their crafts. Also, by allowing the use of a counselor with his own paddle, you've in fact created a case of past precedence, which in turn could be argued that modifications made in the hull material and the internal structure—"

"Silence!" Lutzkraut snapped. "I can't stand listening to your drivel." Then, looking at me, she barked, "Take the canoe! You're already more than eight minutes back. You'll never catch up. I'm heading down the river. And later, at camp, I'll be watching Todd, Magnus, and What's-her-face cross first. The camp will be mine to do with as I see fit. Maybe I'll have the bulldozers get started early . . ."

The thought seemed to lift her spirits and she walked off to join Vanderdick, who was sitting in his Hummer with the motor running, watching us. He had finally arrived with food just after sunrise—greeted by a mixed chorus of boos and cheers.

Steve and Mr. Periwinkle rushed over to help us get situated. Steve said, "You're far behind, but you really do have a chance. This is the finest canoe there is. I made it myself. In just a few strokes, you'll feel the difference."

Mr. Periwinkle added, "And remember what I told you. Be careful when you see the grove of white pine trees on the left bank."

Alison and I looked at each other. "You didn't tell us anything," I informed him. "And what are white pine trees?"

"Well, they're just called that. Eastern white pines, to be exact. Actually they're green." I was getting a headache and was about to ask how we were supposed to tell these trees from all the others in the forest, but he continued talking. "The trees are right before where the river empties into Lake Wy-Mee and the finish line. Stay to the left side when you see the white, I mean green, pines. The river temporarily forks and the right side is named Broke-Neck Rapids for a reason."

"Wait, hold on there." I was suddenly faced with yet another concern. "What's this about breaking my neck?"

Mr. Periwinkle wiggled his hands impatiently. "Nothing to worry about. The river's calm this year . . . except for that unfortunate incident last month with those twelve rafters."

I could feel the blood leaving my face. "But Mr. Periwinkle . . ."

He ignored me and kept talking. "They are, after all, the only Class Six rapids in America—or something like that. Anyway, you're not going down them, and there's a big warning sign. Just stay to the left at the white pine trees, which are actually—"

"Enough!" Steve shouted. "The Algonquins are probably at the camp already. Now git goin'."

He gave us a hard shove off the bank and into the river's current. This time we stayed afloat. Knowing that we'd have to break every canoe-race record, we paddled like demons. I was also aware that Steve hadn't been lying when he said we'd notice a difference. The canoe was super light. It floated higher in the water and glided much more gracefully than the aluminum one. If we'd had it yesterday, we'd have zipped right by the Algonquin boat.

For a little while we toiled along the winding Drownalott River. The day was already getting hot and a bead of sweat dripped down into my eyes. I rubbed it away with my shoulder and kept studying the shoreline. T-Bone had told me to look for an old boathouse on the right. After about twenty minutes, Alison spied it.

"Josh, paddle up to that shack on the water," I said. The boathouse was crumbling into the river. A section of the roof had fallen and was partially submerged, but the walls still stood on the solid rock footing. We were able to paddle right inside of it.

"Is this the finish?" Josh asked. "Did we win?"

"No, this is the shortcut. The back wall of the boathouse should open if we push on it." I paddled the canoe till it bumped quietly against the old rotten wood.

"This place is creepy," Alison said.

I certainly agreed, but I braced the canoe against the fallen roof for leverage and said, "Push!" As the three of us applied muscle, the back wall slid up on rusty hinges, opening just enough for us to paddle under. Even so, we had to bend down in the canoe to squeeze through. Slimy drops of water fell on our hair as we passed under the wall.

"There's the canal, I think," Alison said.

I understood her hesitation. The surface of the water

was completely covered by a green scum, making it look more like a path than a stream. I took my paddle and ladled some of the murk aside. What lay below was brown and smelly, but it was liquid and we could paddle into it. The canal was shallow—I could touch the bottom with my paddle — and only about five feet across. It was pretty straight and led into the overgrown woods.

"Do you think it still connects with the river?" I asked Alison.

"Only one way to find out."

My instincts were naturally screaming to turn around, but Alison seemed up for the adventure. Having her on board was proving to be valuable, especially when she suggested that we could make better time if she helped us push along the bottom and sides of the canal. "I just need to find a big stick."

We made our way to the side of the canal and held the canoe steady while Alison jumped out and looked around on the forest floor. "Hmm. This should work."

She climbed back in with a long, rusty pole that was attached to some rotting wood. We shoved off. It was tough to maneuver at first, since the canal was so narrow, but somehow Steve's canoe seemed to flex through the tight spots and slide easily over submerged logs. I wondered what the canoe was made of.

Leaves and branches hung low above us and we had to push our way through the growth. At times creepy little critters fell onto us. I knocked one large, black bug from the top of Alison's hair before she noticed, and I prayed nothing like it was crawling down my shirt. The thought gave me the heebie-jeebies, and I almost yelled, "Hallelujah!" when I noticed the passage widening up ahead.

Escaping the branches and creepy-crawlies did little to make me feel better when I saw an old collapsing bridge above the canal. On the bridge a boy stared down at us. His skin was very pale, which contrasted drastically with eyes so dark and black that they didn't seem to have pupils. He flashed an unnerving smile of greenish teeth, held up a banjo, and began to play.

The notes sounded sinister on the deserted canal, and we paddled harder. After we passed underneath I looked back. He was still playing and still smiling, but suddenly he shook his head back and forth.

I shivered. Something didn't feel right. T-Bone had warned me about avoiding the locals, but I wondered how you could avoid anyone along this route. It only went one way, and we were like sitting ducks in the canoe. I also realized that nobody in the world had any idea where we were, and traveling down this dark, lonely stretch of water, shortcut or no, was a real bad idea.

"Hi," Josh said. Startled, I looked at the left bank. An old man stood there, his arms hanging straight down at his sides. His clothes hadn't seen laundry detergent in years. Neither smiling nor frowning, he just stared down at us. The blankness of his face was oddly terrifying.

I nodded at him and tried to look pleasant, but through clenched teeth I hissed at Josh, *"Keep paddling."*

"Hi," Josh said again. More people were walking up. Josh was smiling at them. *Of all the times for him to work on his social skills.*

The new arrivals also held blank expressions and wore scraggly, dirty clothes.

"Keep paddling."

Another guy appeared, leading what looked like a mountain lion by a chain.

"Nice kitty," Josh said and held out his hand.

This time it was Alison's turn. *"Keep paddling, Josh."* I could hear the strain in her voice.

Mountain Lion Man growled, "You wanna come over for lunch?"

That made me cringe. What could they possible be serving? *Could it be us?*

"I'm hungry," Josh said.

"No, you're not." Then louder, so that our host could hear, I said, "You know, we'd love to, but we're actually in a race and we have to keep going."

The man's face darkened. He spat some thick brown liquid down on a rock. Alison looked nervously back at me. I could think of only one thing to do.

"Your shoe's untied," I said, looking down and pointing at his feet. His *bare* feet! Not good.

He turned to the growing crowd. "Let's show these folk how we treat uninvited guests." With that, everyone started walking toward us. We were goners. In a flash I thought of my family and friends back home. They were probably playing volleyball at some picnic, while I was about to get eaten by backwoods zombies.

"I'd stop right there if I were you!" The voice was loud and clear—and belonged to Alison. She was standing in the center of the canoe holding up the long metal rod she had used as a paddle. With the piece of wood attached, it was a dead ringer for a hunting rifle—if you were blind. "Let us be on our way and no one gets hurt."

"Sit down, Indiana Jones," I whispered. "And Josh, move it!" I pulled as hard as I could on the paddle and we lurched ahead.

Expecting to see some maniac or mountain lion in hot pursuit, I was afraid to look back, but Alison's bluff seemed to be working. All three of us were now paddling and pushing as fast as we could, and Steve's canoe had taken on a life of its own. Alison looked back and slowly blew out a large breath. Maybe we had escaped after all, but it wasn't until we broke out into the sun and the fresh swirling water of the Drownalott River that I breathed my own sigh of relief.

Being clear of the murky canal, the dense plants, and weird threatening people brought on a wave of joy. I laughed. "Alison, what the heck was that back there? Are you nuts?"

"Hey, you inspired me, the way you scared off those bikers last night. But anyway, I should smack you with your paddle for taking us in there in the first place. That had to be the worst idea ever, Rodney!" She was also laughing now.

I listened, but something held my gaze. "Worst idea ever, huh?"

"Yeah, worst idea ever!"

"Look up there and tell me how bad it was." She spun around and I heard her gasp in disbelief. Todd, Tabitha, and Magnus were within sight. It was clear they hadn't noticed us. They were taking their time. I could see Todd pointing at something in the trees.

"Keep quiet, so we can sneak up to them," I whispered.

"HUH?" Josh yelled.

I cringed and watched helplessly as Magnus turned around. We were just close enough to see his eyes bug out in surprise. I heard him yell, "Goot moovin'!" Their paddles began to hit the water with a renewed fury.

Just like that, it was back to the frantic sprint of the day before. They held the lead and weren't worn out from trying to avoid a hillbilly luncheon, but we had Steve's almost supernatural canoe, and it was clear that we were keeping up with them. Unfortunately, we weren't really gaining ground.

For the next hour or so, we put everything we had into it. Steve's special canoe almost seemed as if it was paddling, too. I could sense the Algonquin team's growing frustration that they couldn't shake us, and I began to think a win was possible. That idea was just the motivation I needed, for the paddling had become the most grueling thing I'd ever experienced. Every part of my body ached and I gasped for each breath. My head swirled from the extreme exertion and I felt an almost dreamlike state come over me. Until Alison broke the silence.

"Look up ahead! I think that's the grove of pine trees Mr. Periwinkle told us about. That's where the river splits."

I did see some pine trees in the distance, but we had passed lots of pine trees. Hoping Alison was right, though, I called to Josh, "Come on. Paddle faster! The finish line should be coming up soon."

While my body struggled with the rigors of the race, my foggy senses soaked in views of the mountains and the sharp, rocky ledges surrounding us on both sides of the river. The shadowy boulders and wildflowers were very cool, and through my exhaustion I remembered once again why it was so important to win. None of this would be left if Vanderdick and Lutzkraut got their way. I even spotted a deer at one point, and a little later a hawk swooped down above us. Rounding out the wildlife visits, a trout jumped out of the water and hit Josh in the side of the head.

"Hey, fishy likes me," he said, turning around. He was smiling, but his head looked kind of slimy.

"That's great. How 'bout paddling now?"

He resumed, and I felt reenergized by our animal cheerleaders. That good feeling lasted until we got closer to the pine trees and I sighted one more creature on the shore. This one was horrible. It looked hideous, with its strangely colored orange hair, evil eyes, and angry mouth. It saw me and clawed savagely at the air.

"Hey, look, there's Mrs. Lutzkraut!" Alison yelled.

She was standing next to a big sign with a red arrow pointing to the right. Under the arrow, wet-looking letters declared: DANGER—KEEP TO RIGHT.

"Didn't Mr. Periwinkle say the rapids were on the right side of the pine trees?" Alison asked.

So much had happened since his early-morning talk, and I had been so confused about the color of the trees, that I couldn't remember for certain. "All I know," I told Alison, "is that I definitely don't trust Mrs. Lutzkraut."

Mr. Cramps had now joined her and the two of them were pointing at us and laughing. For the first time I became aware that the river was starting to move a lot faster. I looked up ahead to see which way Todd and Magnus had gone and with a rush of panic realized that they were nowhere in sight. I had been too busy looking at Cramps and Lutzkraut on the shoreline to notice which course the Algonquins had chosen.

"Nice try, Rodney," Mr. Cramps yelled into a megaphone, "but the best team is about to win!"

He handed the megaphone over to Mrs. Lutzkraut. "You've come mighty close," she shrieked, her voice mixing with a terrifying sound from up ahead—the rapids. We were getting close now, but which way to navigate? Mrs. Lutzkraut continued. "As you can see, you're passing the pine trees and that means Camp Wy-Mee and the finish line are under a mile away. You'll never catch them!"

We were out in the middle of the river. The thunderous roar of the rapids was getting louder by the second. I noticed a subtle current starting to pull us in their direction—to the right. Frantically, I yelled, "Paddle!" I dug my paddle in deep on the right side to push us away. I could see the calm river to the left and couldn't understand why we weren't making any progress reaching it—until I noticed Josh. He was busy paddling on his left, which pushed us ever closer to disaster. "Paddle on the right, Josh!" I yelled. "Right!"

"Yes!" he called back and kept paddling on the left.

"Right!" I shouted. I wasn't sure if he couldn't hear me because of the rapids or if he'd gone completely stupid on us.

"I know. Thanks!" he answered.

Alison got in on the act. "No, Josh. Not right like correct. Right like right!" Seeing that her words only confused him further, she shouted, "Switch sides!"

"Okay!" Josh turned around in his seat so that he faced Alison and me and began paddling backward. I smacked my forehead. By now the canoe was spinning around in circles. I couldn't help but notice Lutzkraut and Cramps on the shoreline hooting with laughter.

Alison screamed, "We're heading into the rapids! I can't swim!"

"I thought you were Miss Doggy-Paddle?" I said, trying one last time to steer us away from certain death. It was no good.

"Rodney, *do* something!"

The canoe slammed into a boulder, and we spun viciously into the fast-moving current. We were done for. I was too scared to do anything other than hang on. It felt like we were on a roller coaster designed by some deranged lunatic who had skipped every safety class at engineering school. We bounced off rocks and crashed down waterfalls. Several times we almost flipped into the churning white water. As I gripped the side, I realized that if we had been in an aluminum canoe, we'd have been crushed like a soda can.

The rushing water was so loud that I couldn't hear Alison's screams or my own. I had been in so many tight spots and experienced so many horribly dangerous moments that I should have been used to it by now. *But no*, I whimpered to myself, *this is the most terrifying of them all.*

That is, except for what happened next.

So much water had splashed into my eyes that I could barely see. I was choking on the spray. I could feel the canoe being pulled ever faster along the surface of the water. I temporarily let go with my right hand and wiped my face. I spotted one last waterfall. It was over ten feet high and I knew we were finished. I tried to yell, "Help!" but a vicious wave blasted into my open mouth.

As I gagged up the water we shot off the ledge, heading—no doubt—for some jagged rocks below. Instead of falling straight down, though, the canoe caught the air and we launched forward, momentarily sailing parallel to the river. We came down seconds later, like a snowboarder nailing a jump. Instead of fine white powder, however, a spray of foam encircled us . . . and to my extreme relief, we came out into the calm of Lake Wy-Mee.

"We're alive!" Alison cheered. "Great paddling, Rodney. You saved us!"

I quickly picked up my paddle off the floor of the canoe. "Er, thanks."

"I can't believe we made it in one piece!" she continued.

"Not only that." I smiled, having spotted something rather spectacular off to my left. "We're winning!" Josh and Alison turned to port and saw that we were at least twenty feet ahead of Todd's shocked face.

"This has been a day of shortcuts." Alison laughed. "And Steve's canoe was amazing the way it floated in the air back there. I wonder what it's made of?"

"Moose guts," Josh said. "He told me about it last night."

Alison and I jumped up and wiped our pants—but only for a second. Something had caught her eye. "It's just ahead!" she shouted. "The finish line. Let's get going."

We clearly had the momentum. Todd and Magnus tried frantically to catch up but were no match for the Moose Mobile. Josh and I were able to easily hold them off. Soaked to the bone, as in a dream, we paddled under the big banner that read FINISH.

The whole camp erupted into cheers. Everyone was jumping up and down on the floating docks calling out our names. Well, almost everyone. Surrounded by six beautiful girls, Fernando was resting in a lounge chair overlooking the lake. Hearing the commotion, he turned in our direction and raised a glass.

Before leaving the canoe, I hugged Alison and called over to Josh, "Hey, buddy, we did it!"

"Did what?" he asked.

"We won, Josh." I laughed.

"Won what?"

"Never mind. High five!"

The following smack nearly broke my hand, but the intense pain didn't dampen my spirits at all. We had won. We had saved Camp Wy-Mee.

Chapter 24

GROUNDBREAKING NEWS

I was soaked, shivering, and completely exhausted as I climbed from the canoe, but it didn't dampen the excitement I felt as a horde of campers and counselors charged onto the dock to greet us. I quickly learned how a college basketball team feels when the student body rushes the court after a championship game. Alison and I had to duck in behind Josh to keep from being crushed or knocked into the water. Kids I hadn't noticed all summer were slapping us on the back, and they all seemed to be shouting at once:

"Way to go!"

"You saved the camp!"

"Amazing!"

"Someone finally beat the Algonquins!"

Perhaps the biggest kid of all pushed his way through the crowd. "Well done, Rodney!" Mr. Periwinkle beamed. "I knew you could do it."

"Really?"

"No, but let's go celebrate."

The pandemonium lasted for at least another hour. Throughout it all I was cheered, tugged, hugged, congratulated, and forced to recount our adventure. It was almost as tiring as the canoe race! Most of it blurs in my mind, with the exception of one mental snapshot.

For a brief second, the crowd parted and I noticed a sour-looking group off to the side. Mr. Vanderdick, Mrs. Lutzkraut, and their henchmen leaned against a table, not speaking. They appeared to be in total shock. Their faces wore an expression of disbelief. Above them, gold and black balloons spelled out VANDERDICK MALL GROUNDBREAKING.

I gave a little wave.

That sure broke their trance. Vanderdick snapped the handle of a gold-plated shovel over his knee and stormed off. Three guys in black suits disappeared among the kids. Lutzkraut, on the other hand, remained motionless. Her eyes—staring deep into mine—flashed a look of horror and hatred.

I didn't dwell on her feelings. Right behind her, I could see that the table was piled high with fancy sandwiches, two big hams, at least five different desserts—you name it. Vanderdick must have had the groundbreaking ceremony catered. I hadn't eaten a real meal in forty-eight hours and my stomach rumbled. As Lutzkraut lifted a glass of champagne to her lips, I turned to my hundred new friends and yelled, "Let's get some food!"

The crowd loved the idea, but not Mrs. Lutzkraut. She dropped the champagne glass and ran screaming from the approaching mob. We surrounded the table and attacked it like a pack of wolves devouring a deer. As I gnawed on some shrimp and a lobster tail, I figured the spread hadn't been meant for us, but I didn't care. It was celebration time and I had earned it.

And the celebration didn't end with a full belly. As the sun lowered in the sky, Mr. Periwinkle announced we'd have a special campfire in honor of the momentous day.

Not too long after that, Josh, Alison, and I found ourselves sitting on the Log of Honor, closest to the crackling fire. It had a great view, but my eyes burned from all the smoke that kept blowing in my face. Directly behind us sat Fernando, Stinky, Thorin, and a group of Alison's friends, who were now packed rather tightly around Fernando. I was pleased to notice that the Algonquins had decided to boycott the campfire and that Lutzkraut and her crew were nowhere in sight.

For entertainment, the counselors performed skits. Woo played the trumpet, and Gertrude and Alice did an interesting, if not a little weird, musical number by banging on a bunch of pots and pans. When they finished, Mr. Periwinkle stepped up to speak.

"As you know, camp ends in two days. Two more days to enjoy everything that Mother Nature has to offer us in this magnificent setting. Of course, we will have many more summers now, thanks to Rodney Rathbone and his canoemates." He pointed our way and there was a round of cheers. Periwinkle waited for the crowd to quiet down. "I want to remind everyone of the last-day-of camp awards ceremony. It's in two days. After your parents have settled in, we will hand out the many summer awards, all leading up to the most important honor—the honor that *you* will decide by camp vote tomorrow. I am referring to none other than the annual naming of King and Queen Wy-Mee."

He paused for a moment, his face becoming more serious. "Yes, it's no ordinary award. As many of you know, the king and queen, under Camp Wy-Mee by-laws, have the power to change one camp rule or influence one camp decision."

Make a camp decision? What was this? They let kids decide policy? I smelled potential disaster and raised my hand.

Periwinkle looked down at me and smiled. "I know what you're thinking, Rodney. It's one of those brilliant rules that distinguishes Camp Wy-Mee from other camps. When we say the opinion of the camper matters, we mean it!" Some people clapped. I began to sweat. Periwinkle continued, "For example, has anyone had to eat Gertrude's salmon loaf this summer?"

"No!" cheered my fellow campers.

Gertrude looked taken aback. Alice pretended to threaten Periwinkle with a wooden spoon and everyone laughed. "Precisely!" he continued. "It's an example of a policy change made by a former camp king and queen . . . after spending an unfortunate night in the infirmary."

I couldn't take it anymore and had to ask the question that was making *me* sick. "Could the king and queen decide to tear down the trees and develop the camp?" I blurted.

Mr. Periwinkle frowned. "I'd have to ask the lawyers, but why on earth would you want to do that?"

"Well, I wouldn't, but what if someone whose father stood to make millions of dollars happened to win?"

Mr. Periwinkle laughed. "Rodney, it's like a big popularity contest. Everyone's going to vote for you." He laughed some more, nervously this time, and turned to the crowd. "Aren't I right?"

"Yeaaahhhhhh!" the crowd screamed before breaking into chants of "ROD-NEY! ROD-NEY! ROD-NEY!"

You would assume hearing the cheers would make me feel pretty good, but as I sat there before the fire I couldn't shake the thought: *What if I don't win?*

When the chants finally died down, Mr. Periwinkle announced, "All right, it's getting late. There's only one more thing to do this summer to complete the ultimate camp experience. It's time for the greatest of all camp traditions . . ."

I noticed Mrs. Periwinkle walking toward us. My mind raced with unlikely camp traditions. Was she about to walk barefoot on burning coals? Reenact someone getting burned at the stake? This was getting interesting . . . until I noticed her take a seat in front of her husband. Mr. Periwinkle gave her a big smile and turned to the rest of us. "Campers, it's time for that great Camp Wy-Mee tradition—a fireside ghost story. Steve . . . ?"

A scary story? This was one camp experience I could do without.

Survival Steve appeared out of the smoke. "I'm going to tell you a story. It's a darn scary one, and it's true, so if you don't think you can take it, you best leave now." I began to rise, but then Steve added, "It's called the Legend of . . . *Greeny*!"

My fellow campers snickered. Someone called, "Oooooooh, Greeny! I'd better cover my ears." Even Stinky, who was scared of just about everything, had a smile on his face. Greeny? How scary could this be? I looked over at Alison and we both smiled. I settled back onto the Log of Honor and decided to enjoy the story. Maybe it would get my mind off of this King Wy-Mee stuff.

Steve's face remained dark as he looked around at each of us. Flames from the fire reflected in his eyes. His voice dropped to a deep, unsettling level. "We'll see how many of you are laughing when the fire dies low, you're alone, and thoughts of Greeeeeny come back to haunt you."

Again there was laughter, although it sounded a bit uneasy.

"The tale starts twenty years ago. A boy, not much older than most of you sitting before me, was arrested. The crime was so gruesome and horrible that I could never live with myself if I described it to you now, but I can tell you that the judge and half the jury that listened to the case went . . . crazy."

He paused. One nervous giggle. I felt my chest begin to tighten. I also felt Alison nestling closer to me. I liked that, although it reminded me of a rather unpleasant memory involving Jessica, a scary movie, and a Coke. At least this time there was no soda for me to spill on Alison.

"The boy," Steve continued, "was sent to Skruloose Asylum for Violent Offenders. The same Skruloose Asylum that isn't too far from Camp Wy-Mee. The boy was so savage and dangerous that they stuck him in the thickest padded cell in the deepest basement. But it wasn't enough. In less than a year he managed to escape."

I glanced behind me. So many girls now clung to Fernando that he looked like a human magnet.

"The manhunt lasted for a whole year. Hundreds of police, bloodhounds, helicopters, and even a psychic failed to find him. He had disappeared into the woods. *These* woods," Steve exclaimed, motioning all around us.

Alison's hand gripped my bicep. Stinky chewed his sweatshirt sleeve. Josh sat with a dopey grin.

"Every now and then people thought they saw him, a boy gradually becoming a man and turning green from living alone, like an animal in the woods. *These* woods. Every now and then a hiker, or a boater, or a *camper* would disappear. Some foolish people said these people just ran away or moved, but deep down everyone knew what had really happened. Greeny got them."

I looked over and realized I was now gripping *Alison's* bicep. *Good thing I'm not holding a Coke*, I thought.

"And then the sightings ended. People stopped going missing and the citizens in the towns around Camp Wy-Mee forgot about Greeny."

That was good, I thought. I took a deep breath.

Survival Steve raised his pointer finger in the smoky air and paused momentarily. "However, the people should have been more careful. They should not have forgotten about Greeny. They should have remembered that he was still out there somewhere, hiding in the woods. Parents should have thought twice about sending their little loved ones off to camp."

My heart was in my throat. Steve leaned down over the fire and took on an orange glow of his own. "Yes, *your* parents should never have sent you here. And you shouldn't be here right now, sitting around this fire. Do you know why?"

No one could answer.

"Because *I'M* Greeny!!" he shouted, leaping right in front of us.

"AHHHHHHHHHHHHHHHHHHHHHHH!" Everyone, except maybe Josh, screamed. Mr. Periwinkle

235

bolted off into the woods. Alison and I flipped back-ward, falling off the log. She landed on me with a thud.

For a second I was in a fear-induced coma, but as I came out of it I realized that someone was actually laughing. I strained my eyes to look up, and there was Steve, tears streaming down his face. "Ha-ha-ha-ha-ha! Boy, that was fun. Nothing like a good ol' ghost story 'round the campfire."

Alison, who was taking her time getting off my chest, said, "Your friend has a weird sense of humor."

"That's one way to describe it," I muttered.

"And look at you, lying there. What about protect-ing me from Greeny?"

"At least I broke your fall."

She smiled at that. "My hero." Then her eyes looked more closely into mine and I felt my heart begin to ham-mer in my chest. "It's kind of sad," she continued. "The end of camp is in two days. After that we go home."

"Uh," I managed to reply.

She kept looking at me expectantly, slowly twirling strands of her red hair. Did she want me to kiss her? Looking at her in the firelight, I wanted to, but another part of me wrestled with the same Jessica questions I had battled all summer. My heart beat faster. My mind grew hazy. Jessica was miles away. I knew I had to . . .

"Would someone please find my husband?" Mrs. Periwinkle demanded. "He's heard that stupid story for nineteen years and runs every time." She noticed us on the ground and asked, "What are you two doing down there? Get up!" Focusing her gaze squarely on Alison, she scolded, "I can tell you one thing, young lady. You'd never catch a nice girl like Rodweena rolling around in the pine needles."

"I wouldn't be so sure of that," Alison said.

Mrs. Periwinkle had broken the mood and saved me from an awkward situation. As she walked off with her friends, Alison gave me a little wave. I waved back. The campfire was over and there was a lot to digest. Needing time to think, I cut away from the crowd of boys heading back to the cabin. I realized that I would soon have to face the decision I'd been avoiding for much of the summer. In two days I'd finally be seeing Jessica. Was she still my girlfriend? There was still a slight chance she was, but Alison . . . I couldn't deny how I felt about her.

My mind was wrestling with the girl dilemma when I rounded out from behind a row of thick pine trees and onto the soccer field. Something caught my eye and stopped me dead in my tracks.

Up on the Periwinkles' balcony, Mrs. Lutzkraut sat rocking slowly in a chair. I could see a smile etched on her face in the moonlight. I stood there watching her rock back and forth. Why was she smiling? Considering that she had just lost her chance to sell the camp, she should have been packed and gone by now. And definitely not smiling—unless, of course, she was planning . . .

Without warning, her head swiveled sharply in my direction. I panicked and dove into the trees, not sure if she saw me. Fear coursed through my entire body. Within the past twenty-four hours I had confronted bikers, slept out on Skull Rock, been chased by zombie hillbillies, barely survived Broke-Neck Rapids, and been scared out of my wits by a ghost story. How much could one coward take?

I didn't stick around to find out. Before Mrs. Lutz-kraut or Greeny or Todd could catch me alone in the woods, I took off at full speed for the one place I felt safe. Loserville.

Chapter 25

UNDER THE OLD BEECH TREE

Awakening from a horrendous nightmare, I flung myself out of bed—still wrapped in my sleeping bag—and tumbled to the cabin floor like some loser in a potato-sack race. Luckily my face broke the fall. When the pain eventually subsided to excruciating, I eyed the room and noticed that everyone seemed to be up and gone already. At least no one had witnessed my nosedive. What had made me jump out of bed like that?

I unzipped the steamy sleeping bag. As the cool morning air rushed in, I lay there trying to remember the nightmare. Staring up at the beams, I noticed a spider watching me from the corner of its web. It was hairy and creepy and reminded me of . . . Mrs. Lutzkraut! That's it! I remembered the dream. Mrs. Lutzkraut had been smiling evilly at me in the moonlight, rocking back and forth in her chair. It was all too horrifying. I exhaled and said aloud, "Thank goodness it was only a . . . crap!"

"Did you have an accident, Rodney?" Stinky asked from the doorway.

"What? No! Wait a second, where is everyone?"

"They're all coming back from breakfast. We decided to let you sleep. You were tossing and turning all night. And hey, don't worry about the accident. I have them all the time. Just the other day, I . . ."

"Frank, did you see Periwinkle? I have to talk to him!"

"I saw him walking to his tree, but I don't think you have to tell him. Just take a shower and change."

"I'll see you later, Frank. Uh, good talk. Remind me never to borrow your shorts . . ."

I left Stinky standing there looking perplexed. My dream was no dream. Lutzkraut had been smiling up on the porch. If there's one thing I'd learned this past year, it's that a happy Lutzkraut is a dangerous Lutzkraut. She had a plan, all right, and I needed to stop it. Warning Periwinkle was the first and most important step.

I dodged most of the campers who tried to congratulate me on the race, but one was a bit more aggressive. Practically tackling me, Tabitha asked, "Rodney, where are you going so fast?"

"I have to take care of something," I panted, trying to step around her.

She blocked my course. "Are you up to one of your adventures?"

I smiled weakly.

"You know," she continued, "that canoe race was amazing. I was in the other canoe and all, but I was rooting for you." She smiled and leaned closer. "I can't believe you went down Broke-Neck Rapids. That's very exciting."

"Yeah, it was. Now I really need—"

She grabbed my hand. "Rodney, I was just on my way to vote for the Camp Wy-Mee king and queen. I'll vote for you, if you vote for me. Wouldn't we make an awesome royal couple?"

"Um, sure. Bet we would. Now I really need to go."

She looked puzzled as I took off around her. A few seconds later she yelled, "Hey!" but I kept moving across the soccer field. The beech tree was in my sights.

As I sprinted up the final steps to the tree, I could see Mr. Periwinkle sitting in a plaid folding chair enjoying his favorite view. I bent over to catch my breath before sputtering, "Mr. Periwinkle"—*gasp*—"Mrs. Lutzkraut"—*gasp*, *gasp*—"she's up to something . . ."

"Of course she's up to something. She's helping to arrange the end-of-summer awards ceremony. Isn't that right, Helga?"

I was still bent over. *Helga*? I raised my eyes.

Just to Periwinkle's left sat his wife and sister-in-law. Mrs. Periwinkle was looking at me with a serious expression, but Lutzkraut wore a devious smirk. She said, "That's right, Percy. I'm helping to make sure that the camp grand finale goes off without a hitch."

Red flags smacked me in the face with each word, but Periwinkle just kept on beaming. "Isn't that wonderful, Rodney? There's a lesson here. Mrs. Lutzkraut suffered a disappointment, but instead of dwelling on it, she's accepted it, embraced our vision for the camp, and offered to help. Truly a noble gesture, wouldn't you agree?"

"No!" I shouted. This was no time for tact. "Mr. Periwinkle, you can't possibly trust her."

"Rodney, that's rather rude. Mrs. Lutzkraut is sitting right here. She was just telling me how she'd been mistaken all along. The money blinded her, and now she sees what's really important. Isn't that true, Helga?"

"That's right, Rodney," she answered, not looking at me but staring straight ahead. "Look out at that view. To think, I almost uprooted acres of poison ivy and killed thousands of innocent mosquitoes, and for what? Millions and millions of dollars? What could I have been thinking?"

Mr. Periwinkle nodded. "Everyone deserves a second chance."

Mrs. Periwinkle kept her mouth shut and tried to look calm, but her eyes told a different story. She was staring at me so intently that she seemed to be trying to see right through me. It was kind of freaky, so I looked back at Mr. Periwinkle. He picked up a glass of lemonade from where it was balanced between two roots, took a long sip, and placed it back on the ground. "I'm just so thrilled you've seen the light, Helga." He smiled.

"Me too, Percy. I can rest easy now knowing that dirty little campers will be scurrying over these grounds for generations to come." Turning to me, she suddenly asked, "Did you vote yet for king and queen? I hear you're the favorite. Just imagine, one of my former students, King Wy-Mee! You have no idea how that makes me feel."

The sarcasm and wickedness dripped off each syllable. My throat was dry. So this was how she intended to destroy the camp. She was going to rig the king and queen elections.

Mr. Periwinkle beamed. "Oh, Helga, this is going to be a glorious end to the summer."

"Glorious will be an understatement," she said, still smiling at me. "It will be the happiest day of my life."

I had to try one last time. "Mr. Periwinkle, there's too much at stake for second chances. Don't you see? She's going to—"

"Now, now, Rodney. Don't be so suspicious. It's bad for the digestion. Helga, reassure poor Rodney that you no longer care about developing Camp Wy-Mee."

"Why, Percy, I'm hurt that you would even suggest such a thing." Her bottom lip began to quiver. "A deal's a deal, and I intend to honor my end of the bargain."

"You see, Rodney? She's the picture of sincerity."

As Mr. Periwinkle leaned over to pick up his lemonade, Miss Sincerity gave me a nasty wink and held up two crossed fingers.

"What?" Mr. Periwinkle barked.

Oh good! He had spotted her. *Now* he'd listen to reason.

"There's an ant in my glass! Little guy is trying to drink my lemonade."

Of course he hadn't seen her. Mrs. Lutzkraut was too good at this.

"I don't blame the little creature," he continued. "Mrs. Periwinkle makes the best lemonade in all Ohio. Don't you, Hagatha?"

I looked at Mrs. Periwinkle. She didn't react to the compliment. Her eyes were still drilling into me.

Mr. Periwinkle gently dropped the ant to the grass. "Next time we'll have to bring a whole pitcher just for the bugs."

Mrs. Periwinkle ignored her husband and asked me, "Who was that you were speaking to down on the field?"

I didn't see the harm in telling the truth. "Tabitha."

The name wiped the smirk right off Lutzkraut's face. She blurted, "Tabitha? Isn't that the one you recommended, Hagatha? If Rodney's got his hooks into her . . ." She caught herself. Although she tried to regain her easy-going, relaxed act, the eye twitch I'd come to know so well had returned. She half mumbled, "We'll talk later." Then, a little more loudly, she spat, "Rodney, I think it's time for you to go."

Still smiling, Mr. Periwinkle said, "Yes, go vote, Rodney, and get some rest tonight. Big day tomorrow."

Well, at least he was right about one thing. Tomorrow would be a big day.

I wandered out onto the fields and did my best to sort things out. I tried all afternoon. Later, though, while brushing my teeth in the bathroom before bed, I realized I hadn't gotten anywhere. Sure, I had an idea of what Lutzkraut was up to, but I didn't know how to stop her. My friends had been no help at all. They just laughed. Woo's advice was to "chill," and he played me some new jazz music. It sounded like a bunch of geese getting run over, so I went looking for Alison, only every time I tried to talk to her there were other kids around. Nope, this time I was definitely on my own. It seemed no one could grasp the obvious—Lutzkraut was prepared to stop at nothing to get her way!

I finished in the bathroom and walked out into the darkening evening. Most campers were already in bed. I was alone on the trail that cut through the pines back to Loserville. I came around one particularly large tree and stopped short. There was something odd about the shadows coming from behind the tree. I snuck off the path and came around the tree from the rear. Todd and Magnus lurked.

"I'm gootin' tired of waitin'," Magnus whispered.

"Just a bit longer," Todd whispered back. "He's gotta come this way soon. It's our last chance to give him a little going-away present."

My instincts had saved me again. I slid back quietly into the dark. Their last chance was blown. I was safe. I relaxed and was just starting to sneak off when an icy hand gripped my shoulder.

"Say nothing. Just listen."

The mystery killer in the dark didn't have to worry. I was too terrified to even gasp. The hand spun me around so I could see my end. A faint light from the moon revealed Mrs. Periwinkle's face. It brought little relief. She growled quietly, "I've been looking all over for you. We need to talk."

My heart pounded in my chest but I managed, "You could have waited until breakfast."

"No, I couldn't," she hissed. "We can't be seen together, and we haven't much time."

This was almost as scary as her icy hand. I squeaked, "Why? What's going on?"

"Your suspicions earlier today were justified. My sister's going to change the election results so that you lose. We have only one chance to save the camp, and you're that chance."

Something wasn't making sense. "Mrs. Periwinkle," I asked, "I thought you didn't want the camp saved? I thought you wanted all that money."

"Oh, that doesn't matter anymore. I was wrong. What matters is that I'm desperate. I need to know if I can depend on you. I need to know: Can I count on your help . . . *Rodweena*?"

Chapter 26

THE TRUTH REVEALED

As I rolled up my sleeping bag for the last time, I knew it would be a day of good-byes. A sour kind of sadness squeezed my gut. I'd miss this place. I'd miss my friends. I'd miss the lake and the trails—even Harry the Racoon.

I looked around at my friends. We'd be going to the awards ceremony soon, but this would be the last time we'd be together in the cabin. Without saying anything, we realized it was time for good byes.

Fernando handed Stinky his best bottle of cologne. "Here, you need this more than me."

"Thanks, Fernando!"

Thorin came up to me and gave me a book. "It's *The Hobbit*, by J.R.R. Tolkien . . . my favorite."

"Thanks," I said. "I'll be sure to read it."

"It will change you. Might make you more like me."

I said, "One can only hope."

Thorin turned to Josh. "This one's for you." It was *Green Eggs and Ham*.

Josh opened it up and began to read the first page. "I am Sam. Sam I am." Suddenly he stopped. "This book is broken. I am Josh, not Sam!" He threw it down and put Thorin in a thank-you headlock. I watched the two of them wrestle for a moment.

Fernando walked over. Looking at them, he said, "You can't go wrong with the classics." Then he turned to me. "And so it ends. We had a pretty good run. The ladies, they loved us. You must have some Latin blood in you."

I thought of Aunt Evelyn and how she loved to mambo. "It's possible."

"Rodney, it was an honor and a privilege being your friend. If you're ever in Canton, give me a call." He gave me a slight bow.

"Yeah, I will. I'm not sure I would have made it this summer without you," I said, shaking his hand.

He smiled. "We'll have to do it again next year."

I smiled back, but his words cooled the warm moment. There was a very good chance there wouldn't be a next year.

I went to the wall and began pulling off pictures that I'd hung. I tried to get excited that my parents were on their way to Camp Wy-Mee to pick me up. Then I tried to feel happy that I might even be seeing Jessica when I got home tonight.

Then I stopped pretending. This was no good. Try as I might, I couldn't fight it off any longer. All morning, one emotion had reigned above the others. It was even stronger than the sadness about leaving my friends.

It was fear.

It was the last day, and somewhere out there, while I packed my dirty underwear into my trunk, an evil mastermind was plotting. Somehow once again it had fallen onto my narrow shoulders to stop her. Last night in the woods, Mrs. Periwinkle had outlined perhaps the most ludicrous plan I'd ever heard. Before I could argue and tell her it wouldn't work, she disappeared into the dark like a chubby ninja.

My thoughts were interrupted as a group of counselors marched into the cabin, grabbed our trunks, and loaded them onto a cart. Fernando's trunk seemed to be giving them the most trouble. You could see it was heavy. Suddenly it fell with a crash.

"Hey, easy with the products!" he yelled. "I have to look good for the girls back home."

I sure was going to miss him.

We stepped out of the cabin to walk down to the soccer field for the last time. Woo called, "You've been a group of cool cats this warm verano. Time to drift on out." He put his trumpet up to his lips and played a slow, sweet song. We could hear the notes wafting gently through the hot end-of-August air as we met up with the other boys' cabins and headed off to the ceremony.

When we got to the soccer field I couldn't believe how great it looked. The place was loaded with parents, who cheered and waved as we approached. On the other side of them, I could see the girls approaching. There was a big farewell banner over an awards platform set up on the hill leading up to the Periwinkles' house. Both Periwinkles and Mrs. Lutzkraut were already stationed on it. My stomach tightened at the sight of them. I was never going to be able to pull off Mrs. Periwinkle's plan.

The parents were sitting on the field and a space was reserved for the campers. Mrs. Periwinkle's voice boomed over the loudspeaker. "I know many of you want to see your loved ones, but we're rather behind schedule. The hellos and hugs will need to wait until after the awards cere—"

She stopped speaking. One parent was ignoring her. He ran through the crowd yelling, "Rodney, where are you?"

"Over here, Dad!" He ran up to me and gave me a hug. Seeing this, many of the other parents ran out to hug their children, and it was some time before the ceremony could begin. My mom joined us and also gave me a big hug. She said, "Rodney, we've missed you so much. We can't wait to hear all about it." Then, to my dad, she scolded, "We've been asked to sit down. Come on, Donald."

"Is Penny here?" I asked.

"Your sister had to go to the bathroom." With a smile, my mom added, "Someone took her who I know you'll be excited to see."

"Is it Au—"

"*We're* not telling," my dad cut me off. "We know how you love surprises. I was just reminding your mother how stunned and excited you were two months ago when we told you about coming here. Don't you—"

"Donald, we have to take our seats! See you soon, sweetie."

I went and found where my cabinmates were already sitting on the grass. It felt great seeing my parents, but they weren't going to surprise me. *This time* I was sure Aunt Evelyn had made the trip.

I looked up at the platform. Mrs. Periwinkle still held the microphone. "Thank you for your considerate cooperation." She glanced my way for a moment before handing the microphone to Mr. Periwinkle.

He wore his favorite pith helmet and his smile was wider than ever. "It is a glorious morning. A glorious end to a glorious summer. And what could be more glorious than a final awards ceremony, where we award the glorious achievement of your—"

"Yes! *Glorious.* We get it!" snapped Mrs. Lutzkraut over his shoulder into the microphone. "Many people have long drives ahead of them this afternoon, so let's get a move on with this glorious event."

"Of course, of course." Mr. Periwinkle motioned

toward Lutzkraut and spoke to the parents seated before him. "I'm sure you all know our codirector and my lovely sister-in-law, Helga Lutzkraut." Several suppressed coughs and a couple of lethargic claps rose from the audience.

For the next fifteen minutes, Periwinkle announced the award winners. The awards ranged from the standards, like best swimmer and best artist, to the more bizarre, like loudest whistler and most enthusiastic vegetable eater.

The only time I really focused was when Josh won for best camp spirit. He walked across the platform to receive his medal and Periwinkle asked, "Being our most enthusiastic camper, do you have anything you want to say about Camp Wy-Mee?"

"This camp is, uhh, good."

Mr. Periwinkle clapped and turned to the crowd. "Did you hear that everyone? A modern-day Longfellow. Josh, may we use that in next year's brochure?"

Josh took his medal off. "You want to use this in your brochure?"

"Ha-ha, I love your wit! Okay, go have a seat now." We all clapped and Josh eventually found his way back to us.

"Now for the moment we've all been waiting for," Mr. Periwinkle suddenly announced. My heart began beating faster. "Here at Camp Wy-Mee, we continually strive to make this the best camp experience in the nation. One way we try to achieve greatness is with the crowning of King and Queen Wy-Mee. You see, the king and queen get to create, or alter, one camp policy. The only rule is that the two of them must agree on the decision. No other camp does this. Not Camp Hiawatha, not Camp Granada, not Camp Walden, not Camp North Star, and not Camp Crystal Lake!"

"There's a good reason they don't," I growled, unable to help myself.

Someone in back of me said, "Shhhh!"

After smiling for another minute, Periwinkle added, "This year, Mrs. Lutzkraut was kind enough to run the voting." A bead of sweat ran down my back.

Mrs. Lutzkraut smiled and took the mic. Another bead of sweat ran down. I knew what was coming—I just didn't know if I was brave enough to do what Mrs. Periwinkle expected of me.

"I want to let you know," Mrs. Lutzkraut droned on, "that Mr. Cramps and our gifted, handsome counselor Magnus personally triple-checked the ballots. They then sealed the results in two envelopes. I'm as ignorant as you as to the winners." I doubted that. "Please bring them out."

Magnus walked out and handed the letters to her. By now my shorts were getting soggy from the waterfall pouring down my back.

"I'll announce the king first . . ."

"ROD-NEY!—ROD-NEY! ROD-NEY!" All around

me, campers began to chant. I looked up at my parents. My father was smiling proudly.

Mrs. Lutzkraut scowled and eventually the "Rodneys" faded. "As I was trying to say, the Camp Wy-Mee king *should* be a young gentleman who epitomizes proper behavior, possesses exemplary leadership skills, and will no doubt go on to great things. This year's winner is . . ." She tore open the envelope and made a fake look of surprise. "Todd Vanderdick!" The crowd groaned and gasped, and one parent booed until his wife elbowed him.

Unlike everyone else, I had expected the moment, but it was still hard to take. Mrs. Lutzkraut's plan was moving along. Now there was no doubt. If Camp Wy-Mee was going to be preserved for future generations, it was up to me to save it, and I knew I had to act in the next minute. Suddenly both my legs began shaking. I doubted I would even be able to stand.

Todd, however, had no problem standing up. He jumped to his feet and clasped both hands over his head in victory. There was a smattering of applause from Mr. Vanderdick, his lawyers, and some polite parents who didn't understand that Mr. Creepy was our new king.

Todd made it a point to walk past me on the way up. "You better behave, Rathbone, or I might have your head lopped off." The thought clearly pleased him, but then his face turned harder and more sinister. "You know what? Keep your head. I'm going to use my power

254

in *other* ways. And I'm sure that whoever the queen is, she'll agree." He winked over at Tabitha. She smiled and adjusted an imaginary crown on her head. "You see? My queen is all set." He gave me a stinging pat on the back and walked up to the platform.

Stinky said, "That's weird. I thought you were going to win, Rodney."

I didn't respond. I watched Mrs. Lutzkraut take the second envelope from Magnus. She shot a quick look at her sister. Mrs. Periwinkle's attention was fixed on me.

Mrs. Lutzkraut continued. "Now, for the Camp Wy-Mee queen." Mrs. Periwinkle's eyes looked like they were going to pop out of her head. She mouthed the words, "Now! Go!" I looked away and pretended not to notice.

Mrs. Lutzkraut opened the envelope and smiled. "I have heard a lot about this young lady this summer. I know you made a wise and excellent choice in her." Tabitha stood up and straightened out her summer dress. "The winning young lady is . . . Rodweena Raauhhh-smith. Rodweena, please come up here."

Tabitha stomped her foot and sat down. Alison looked at me, shocked. Fernando, for the first time all summer, lost his cool. He blurted, "Did she just say Rodweena? That can't be possible."

My heart was pounding so hard that I was surprised the microphone on the stage didn't pick it up. It was now or never. If I went through with the crazy plan, I'd be embarrassed in front of hundreds of parents and my fellow campers, face a lifetime of jokes that I could never live down, and possibly be arrested for impersonating a nonexistent person.

Well, I guess no one ever said being a hero was easy! I got up and bolted out of the crowd and around the side of the dining hall. I heard Todd call, "That's it, Rathbone. Run away, you sore loser."

Mrs. Lutzkraut blurted, "Typical." And if she said more, I didn't hear her. I was now around the side of the dining hall, out of sight from the crowd, searching frantically under the stairs. I crawled about and eventually stumbled onto what I'd been looking for. As my fingers clenched the soft material and something hairy, I smiled to myself. Superman sure had it easy compared to me.

"Rodweena!" I could hear Mrs. Lutzkraut shouting into the microphone. "Rodweena, if you don't step up to the stage, we'll have to select another queen."

"Good idea! Don't wait!" yelled a certain brunette.

Mrs. Lutzkraut ignored her and called one more time. "Rodweena!"

"I'm sorry, Mrs. Lutzkraut. I had stepped out for some shade," I called in my high-pitched voice as I made my way back through the crowd.

"Oh, there you are. Wonderful! Come on up." Mrs. Lutzkraut looked relieved. Tabitha stuck her tongue out as I climbed the steps onto the platform. Todd glanced at me, winked, and gave me a sickening smile. Lutzkraut moved away from the microphone and came over to me. "I was beginning to worry . . . Rodweena. Oh my. What happened to your hair . . . and your *dress*?" I looked down. The dress was covered with dirt. A month spent under the steps wasn't exactly a visit to the drycleaner.

I thought fast. "Mrs. Lutzkraut, I'm sorry. I was walking back when I heard my name called and this *awful* boy came tearing around the side of the dining hall and knocked me to the ground!"

"Are you all right?"

"I think so." I held my chest and continued, "It was very traumatic."

"I'm sure it was, and I think we know which boy did that to you." As she said this, her face scrunched up as if she'd just sucked a whole lemon. "Well, never mind that now. Even in a dirty dress you are still the finest young lady in the camp." She walked back to the microphone. "Rodweena has made it!"

There were some muffled cheers. I looked down at my friends and gave them a little wave. They were all in shock, except for Josh, who was blushing and fixing his hair.

Mrs. Lutzkraut said, "I want you to stop for a moment and gaze up here at this fine young gentleman and proper young lady. These are exactly the types of people we are looking for at this camp."

While she talked, Todd whispered in my ear, "I'm surprised we haven't met before. Better late than never."

He gave me a sly smile and said, "Did you know my dad has a yacht?" He nodded as if to answer his own question. I noticed his arm reaching to take mine.

"What kind of girl do you *take* me for?" I gasped, swatting his hand away.

Mrs. Lutzkraut turned back to us and announced, "Once I place these crowns on your heads you will be the official Camp Wy-Mee king and queen." There was some applause again from the Vanderdicks—and now my friends, who knew something was up.

Lutzkraut placed the crown on Todd's head. Todd wasted no time. "With my power as king, I say we demolish the camp and build the biggest megamall this side of the Mississippi!"

"Noo!" gasped Mr. Periwinkle.

"Oh yessss!" hissed Mrs. Lutzkraut, careful to step away from the microphone so no one could hear. "You thought you could defeat me? Your little friend Rodney has already run off. As soon as I place this crown on Rodweena's head and she gives the go-ahead, that bulldozer over there"—she pointed to a tarp that some of Vanderdick's men were removing to reveal a gleaming yellow dozer—"is leveling this place! Come here, Rodweena."

We moved to the edge of the platform in front of the microphone. She carefully placed the crown on my tangled, muddy wig. I looked around for a moment, actually enjoying my coronation. After all, it's not everyday you get crowned queen. Then I said into the microphone,

"With my power as Queen Wy-Mee, I say . . . *I say* . . ."

"Yes? What do you say?" Lutzkraut burst out.

"I say, we give Gertrude's salmon loaf one more try!"

Gertrude yelled, "Hurray!"

"What?" Someone else didn't seem to like my plan. "You're supposed to develop the camp," Mrs. Lutzkraut hissed so that no one could hear. "I was assured you would play ball. Enough joking around. Tell everyone that you want to develop the camp."

"Nope, I don't think I will." I approached the microphone. "Salmon loaf for everyone!"

"What?" Lutzkraut rounded on her sister. "You said she was the perfect choice!"

In the commotion she didn't notice me drag the microphone to where she was yelling. What came out next boomed so loud that you could hear it echo off the faraway hills: "THERE'S NO WAY VANDERDICK AND I WENT TO ALL THE TROUBLE OF RIGGING THIS ELECTION FOR SOME CRUMMY SALMON LOAF!"

Her deafening roar was followed by deafening silence. Half the parents were holding their hands up to their ears. Vanderdick's attorneys could be seen scattering in all directions. Slowly, Lutzkraut turned away from her sister, looked out at the audience, realized what had just happened, and turned her gaze to me. She was crazed. I smiled, knowing that her public admission of the rigged election meant that the camp was finally, truly saved.

Seeing me standing there with a grin did little to help her calm down. "Recount!" she screamed. "Recount! Give me back that crown!"

I didn't have time to react. She swung toward me and gripped the crown, yanking it off my head. She got more than she bargained for. Strands of the wig were tangled in the crown, and it came right off in her hand.

The crowd let out a gasp. Mr. Periwinkle fainted. I didn't have time to look about and soak in the various reactions. Mrs. Lutzkraut's face had turned bright red and looked ready to explode. "YOU? RATHBONE?!!!!" It was the craziest I'd ever seen her and I prepared to defend myself from an attack, but all she could do at this point was shake up and down and tear the Rodweena wig to tatters. She turned on her sister. "He can't do this! He doesn't have the power."

"Actually, he does," Mrs. Periwinkle said. I noticed her husband open one eye. Mrs. Periwinkle held up the rulebook and waved it slowly in the air. For the first time, I saw that Survival Steve was standing to the side of the stage. He gave her a big thumbs up.

"It's good to be the queen," I said to no one in particular.

Lutzkraut looked back and forth from me to her sister. Mrs. Periwinkle tried to calm her. "I'm sorry, Helga, but Percy was right all along. I see that now. This place *is* special."

"Special my—"

The microphone erupted in feedback. Mrs. Lutzkraut kept on screaming. "This place is insane! I knew when you married him"—she looked at Periwinkle pretending to sleep on the stage—"that I inherited all the intelligence in the family, but now, now . . . ARRRRRgghhhhhh-hhhh!" She howled, jumped off the platform, and with surprising agility stormed off into the woods.

By now the assembled crowd was beginning to understand what had just happened. There was some cheering, followed by the "Rodney" chants. I started to walk over to Periwinkle to tell him it was safe to get up but was met by a hard shoulder. Todd stood before me, with Magnus just behind him. He growled, "I hate you!"

"Does this mean I'm not invited on the yacht?" I asked. That only got him madder. His fingers tightened into a fist.

"You wouldn't hit a girl, would you?" He looked mad enough that he probably would, and I knew I was in trouble, but before he could do anything a booming rumble sounded from behind the Periwinkles' house. It was so deafening that Mr. Periwinkle sat up and turned to see.

It was an alarming sight. The Vanderdick bulldozer was moving toward us. Mrs. Lutzkraut was at the controls, laughing wildly. Seeing us she screamed loudly over the engine noise, "You think you can ruin all my plans? Well, now I'm going to ruin something of yours. This camp needs more parking! Say good-bye to your precious beech tree!"

"Noooooooo!" Mr. Periwinkle wailed. "We have to stop her!"

How do you stop a bulldozer? I wondered. The great tree looked doomed.

The bulldozer rumbled right by the platform. Mrs. Lutzkraut leered down at us and with a cackling laugh screeched, "Full speed ahead!"

I watched her push down on a control stick. Instead of gaining speed, the dozer turned sharply to the right. Trying to turn it back, Lutzkraut pulled hard on another lever. Hundreds of campers and parents were running in every direction. With a cloud of black smoke blasting into the sky from the exhaust, the yellow monster shot forth at an amazing rate.

Now it was Todd's turn to yell, "Nooooooo!" I doubted he cared much about the beech tree and I craned my neck to see what lay in the dozer's new path.

"I can't control it!" Mrs. Lutzkraut called out. "Help!"

The next thing I heard was a loud smash, followed by the sound of breaking wood. The bulldozer had finally come to a stop—in the middle of the Algonquin cabin.

Unfortunately, no one was hurt. Just in case, an ambulance was called for Mrs. Lutzkraut, but she eventually climbed down from the dozer by herself. The EMTs tried to put her on a stretcher as she ranted and raved. After finally getting her into the ambulance, I heard one of the drivers call to the other, "We'd better head straight to Skruloose with this one."

"Don't worry, Rodney," Mr. Periwinkle assured me. "She just needs a little rest and relaxation, and she'll get plenty of it where she's going."

I didn't have time to reflect on that. My friends were climbing on the stage and talking all at once. I quickly tore off the Rodweena dress—it felt good to be back in just my shorts and T-shirt—and for a few minutes I got caught up in the usual exciting euphoria of having just defeated the enemy. I had won again! Camp was over and so was the greatest summer of my life. Full of confidence, I smiled. Nothing could bring me down now.

I turned to rejoin the fun, but my attention was immediately seized by something wonderful. Three gorgeous beauties were running rapidly toward me with arms outstretched. For a moment I truly believed I was in heaven, but then my eyes recognized their faces and a stark realization hit me. I was in big trouble. Three girls? What was Jessica doing here?

The girls were so completely focused on me that they didn't see each other until *clunk!* Their heads banged and all three fell to the platform directly in front of where I stood. Rubbing their bumps, they focused on each other. "What are you doing here?" they yelled. "What are *you* doing here?" I was startled, shocked—and a bit thrilled—to hear the same reply from each: "I'm Rodney's girlfriend!"

As their collective words soaked in, Tabitha, Alison, *and Jessica* stared up at me. Jessica and Alison looked horror-stricken, while Tabitha's face formed a slight smirk.

"Uhh-uhh." I let out a nervous laugh, sounding a lot like Mr. Periwinkle. My brain was swimming. I couldn't think of what to do next. What could I possibly say to clear this up? Who should I help up first? I stood frozen, realizing my *glorious* summer couldn't have ended any worse.

"Look at him, honey," I heard my dad say as he made his way through the commotion. I turned my head groggily. My mom was just behind him. My dad continued, "Didn't I tell you how he loves surprises? Rodney, wasn't it great to see Jessica? I knew bringing her here with us was a fantastic idea."

"Uhhhh . . ."

He laughed. "And I know that you'll be equally excited about the other big surprise we have for you."

My mother beamed. "Rodney, we've been dying to tell you! Your father got a new job while you were away. Allow me to introduce you to the new Vice President of Development at Vanderdick Enterprises!"

I could barely hear her voice as I collapsed and fell from the platform.

"You see, sweetie?" my dad added. "I *told* you he loves surprises."